BAA-BAA DEAD SHEEP

"Baa-Baa knows Auntie Gina'd tell Dad. Why does she like him? He spoils everything!" Tears glittered in Cheryl's eyes again.

Gary moved suddenly and kicked an empty paint bucket. It spun across the scene dock and crashed into the far wall. His anger flared up quickly and needed violent expression. Cheryl stole a glance at him. There was an expression on her face that Beth couldn't read, but it quickly vanished.

Toby spoke quietly. "Someone's got to stop that man," he said. He had gone quite pale. Beth sensed that beneath his controlled voice he was dangerously angry. She looked at his mouth set in a line above his firm chin and her heart gave a jump.

"He needs a lesson."

Gary said, "One he won't forget in a hurry . . ."

POINT CRIME

BAA BAA DEAD SHEEP

Jill Bennett

Cover illustration by David Wyatt

Scholastic Children's Books,
Scholastic Publications Ltd,
7–9 Pratt Street, London NW1 0AE, UK

Scholastic Inc.,
730 Broadway, New York, NY 10003, USA

Scholastic Canada Ltd,
123 Newkirk Road, Richmond Hill,
Ontario, Canada L4C 3G5

Ashton Scholastic Pty Ltd,
P O Box 579, Gosford, New South Wales,
Australia

Ashton Scholastic Ltd,
Private Bag 1, Penrose, Auckland,
New Zealand

First published by Scholastic Publications, 1993
Copyright © Jill Bennett, 1993
Cover illustration copyright © David Wyatt, 1993

ISBN 0 590 55309 7

Typeset by TW Typesetting, Midsomer Norton, Avon
Printed by Cox & Wyman Ltd, Reading, Berks

10 9 8 7 6 5 4 3 2 1

1

"What's happened to the blood?"

Beth Greene leaned over the iron railing of the props gallery and called to the two boys in the scene dock just below her.

Toby didn't look up. "Any minute now," he shouted into the bucket that stood on the floor. Gary was stirring the contents with a broken broom handle, pushing his glasses up on his nose with one hand and wielding the stick with the other. Both boys were totally absorbed.

"Well, give me a yell when it's done. Jo's going to need some for the costumes and I want to cross it off my list." Beth ran her biro down the piece of paper she was holding, ticking as she went. She scanned the shelves crowded with props on the wall of the narrow gallery that ran along one end of the theatre scene dock. They were piled high with objects of every sort. Masks hung in bunches from hooks on the walls and underneath the shelves cupboards bulged with things made for long-forgotten plays, waiting to be recycled into something else needed for a new production.

She pounced on an old lacquered tray, put the group of assorted objects she had collected onto it, and prepared to leave the gallery. These were properties to be used for the rehearsal taking place on the stage one floor above them: a lady's fan for Act One, glasses and an old chipped decanter for the second scene and an assortment of books, hairbrushes and cutlery. Beth was the stage manager for the play and all this was her responsibility.

"Beth, come take a look!" Toby still didn't turn round. "Gary's poured in a load of vermilion and I think he's wrecked it."

Balancing her tray, Beth made her way gingerly down the iron steps that linked the gallery to the wider space of the scene dock. She peered into the bucket.

"I've never seen orange blood before," she said.

"Told you!" Toby sat back on his heels and glared at Gary. "You never listen. I said vermilion would make it orange."

"But . . ." Gary dropped the broom handle and held his finger in the air dramatically, "now for my secret ingredient!" He reached for one of the pots of paint standing on the floor close by.

"That's black, you thickhead!"

"Oh, Tobias of little faith!" Gary chanted and proceeded to dribble thick black paint into the half-full bucket.

Toby reached out an arm to stop him but Beth smiled. "Give up, Toby," she said. "You don't stand a chance."

The three of them watched, mesmerized, as the broom handle stirred the strands of black into the waiting paint. Gradually the colour darkened and the brilliant red dimmed to a rich rust.

"It's gone dead now. It's nowhere near blood."

"Well said!" Beth laughed at Toby and he grinned.

"You know what I mean. Just go away before you drop those antique treasures in the bucket. Aren't they wanted on stage? Paula probably thinks you've been gobbled up by the resident ghost by now!"

"And now—" Before Beth could reply Gary was holding another pot of paint high over his head. "Now for my moment of triumph!" His voice soared.

"He does a good imitation of an actor for some-one who only knows how to pull a switch," Toby murmured, raising a superior eyebrow.

He was a leading actor in the youth group

known as SAPS, short for Saplings. Their theatre, The Tree, had been a central part of their lives since most of them had been at the local primary school. All the group agreed they'd rather be called a SAP than a Sapling – a relic from the more romantic nineteen-thirties. No one knew or even cared about the Victorian actor-manager who had given his name to the theatre itself. Now it was just The Tree and Gary was the SAPS' lighting wizard.

Toby's sarcasm sailed over Gary's head as he lowered the small pot to the lip of the bucket. With great deliberation he allowed a drop of start-ling cerise paint to fall into the centre of the thick liquid.

Shutting his eyes he began to stir, chanting,

> "*Bubble, bubble, toil and trouble,*
> *Fire burn and cauldron bubble. . !*"

Toby leaped on him. Taken by surprise Gary sprawled backwards onto the dusty floor of the scene dock as Toby sat on his chest, pinning down his arms.

"You great steaming idiot!" he shouted. "Now you're quoting from 'The Scottish King'. Do you want trouble? Do you want to get us all hurt or something?"

Beth sighed. Their year had been doing *Macbeth* for the exams. Its haunting lines had dominated the summer term. The old superstition about anyone

4

quoting from the play in a theatre was a powerful one. So many stories surrounded it – stories of disaster or death. Even to say the play's proper title was unlucky. She shivered a little.

"OK, Gary, get up!" she said. "You know the routine. Go out, turn around three times and then knock."

"And don't think we'll let you in again." Toby was unforgiving.

Gary dusted himself off. "Just take a look at the blood," he said very smugly.

The colour was perfect.

"Get OUT!" The two others glared at him.

Pushing his glasses up his nose with a gesture of disdain, Gary moved towards the door. Suddenly he stopped and put his hand to his ear. With a gleam in his eye he turned back to Beth and Toby and said deliberately,

"By the pricking of my thumbs something wicked this way comes . . ."

Both of them gasped as he intoned the witch's lines from *Macbeth* with relish. Then the scene dock door flew open with a crash and Cheryl stormed in. Her face was flaming.

"I'll kill him! I'll really kill him!" she shouted.

"Told you!" Gary said.

"Don't you laugh at me, Gary Smith!" Cheryl swung round to face him and Beth caught the glitter of tears in her eyes. This was more than one of Cheryl's hysterical 'moments', she thought. The girl's cheeks were flaming and her breath came in quick gasps.

Beth put her tray of stage props down on the floor. The rehearsal upstairs would have to wait for them a little longer – this looked serious.

"Just calm down, Cheryl," she said, "and tell us."

"It's that man again. I know it is." Toby's voice was flat. "What's he done this time, Cher?"

"He's such a pig!" Cheryl's voice cracked and she sounded like a little girl.

"Never heard of a pig going 'baa-baa!'," said Gary.

"Shut up, Gary!" Beth was exasperated. Sometimes he just didn't know when to stop.

She went across to Cheryl and made her sit on one of the scene dock's work benches.

"Never mind the sawdust, just tell us all about it," she said, sitting down beside her and smiling encouragingly.

Cheryl took a gulp of air, sniffed and rubbed her nose. "You know it was Friday last night, right?" Her voice wobbled a little.

"Right," they agreed.

"And we all went to Jo's for her party, right?" Cheryl hesitated.

"Right," they prompted her.

"And I changed into my new outfit here before we went, and – and Mr Lamb saw me."

Gary had moved closer to her. "So, he saw you. You looked fine to me."

Cheryl, always aware of admiration, glimmered a little at him. "Well, you see," she spoke calmly at last, "it's not what – I mean, my mum and dad don't like – oh, you know . . ." she appealed to Beth.

"You mean," said Beth, the light beginning to dawn, "your parents haven't seen your new gear and wouldn't like it if they did?"

Cheryl grinned in spite of herself. "They'd have a fit," she said.

Beth remembered. Cheryl, small and blonde with her hair falling in ripples over one eye, had danced the night away in a black skirt that was too short to be taken seriously and a shiny white blouse that slipped easily off one shoulder. Beth had envied her. Not her obvious good looks, but the sparkle and high spirits that shone through the brashness of her dress and made her look like a child who had strayed into a grown-up party. The child, Beth thought a little grimly, that her mother and father wanted her to be for ever.

Cheryl's father was a Baptist elder and her mother worked alongside him, busy and caring. Beth liked them both. She wished they would accept Cheryl as she was and not try to make her into someone they thought she ought to be.

"You know how Dad feels about me being a

SAP." Cheryl had calmed down now but her voice became anxious. "He'd stop me just like that," she clicked her fingers, "if he thought it wasn't good for me. He's never understood the theatre – and I just couldn't live without it." Her blue eyes filled with tears.

There was silence for a moment. Cheryl's words sounded over-dramatic but all of them understood and felt very much the same. Life without The Tree and each other would be too empty for words.

Toby broke the spell. "Where does the dear little baa-lamb of The Tree come into all this?" he asked.

George Lamb, resident caretaker of the theatre, was a man in his late forties. No one in the theatre liked him. All the SAPS treated him with wary politeness, but spoke their minds about him behind his back. He held the keys to every door and cupboard in The Tree and had charge of all the theatre's equipment, from Gary's precious lighting box with its complicated circuits to the bags and tins of scene paints. Every brush, every plug came under his authority. Only the kettle in the green room and the coffee Paula Barton brought in seemed free of his heavy hand.

Cheryl sighed. "I bumped into him just now. He was coming out of the boiler room when I was coming out of the loos." She pulled a face. "He bumped into me and pressed me against the wall, by mistake on purpose – he's disgusting!" She shuddered. "He leered at me and said how much he liked my party dress. He thought my Auntie Gina would like it too. He said he was meeting her in the pub tonight and felt sure she'd be interested in what I wore, especially when it made me look so—" she stopped, her face reddening. "He knows she'd tell Dad. Why does she like him? He spoils everything!" Tears glittered in her eyes again.

Gary moved suddenly and kicked an empty paint bucket. It spun across the scene dock and crashed into the far wall. His anger flared up quickly and needed violent expression. Cheryl stole a glance at him. There was an expression on her face that Beth couldn't read, but it quickly vanished.

Toby spoke quietly. "Someone's got to stop that man," he said. He had gone quite pale. Beth sensed that beneath his controlled voice he was dangerously angry. She looked at his mouth set in a line above his firm chin, and her heart gave a jump.

"He needs a lesson."

"One he won't forget in a hurry," Gary added.

"Yeah, yeah, YEAH!" Cheryl breathed it out in one breath, her eyes glittering with hate.

Beth bent to pick up the tray of props. Lamb was a monster, that was true, but she didn't think there was a lot they could do about it. Anyway, she had to go.

"I've got it! I know how we could do it!" Excitement lifted Toby's voice. "But it needs a sacrifice, Gary. A blood sacrifice."

"Sounds about right," Gary said grimly.

Crash! The scene dock door swung back again and Sam Forrest bounced in, breaking the mood. He saw Beth at once and fell on both knees in front of her, touching the floor with his forehead.

He began to chant, "Oh Moon of the World and Jewel of the Galaxy, your humble subjects await your presence!" Then he sat back on his heels and without pausing went into his "camp" routine. "In other words, dear," he flicked his wrist at her, "if you aren't upstairs with your tray of goodies in two seconds flat Paula will have your liver and lights on toast!"

He looked around to see what effect his entrance had made on the others. They stared at him, unsmiling.

"Hello," he said in his ordinary voice. "I sense a plot. What's up?"

"You're a fool, Sam Forrest," Beth said mildly. "I'm gone. Don't forget to let Jo have some blood," she tossed over her shoulder as she pushed her way through the scene dock doors and left them to it.

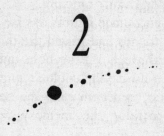

2

The Tree was a small, intimate theatre. It had been built during the time of the Regency when Tolford Regis's popularity was at its height as a fashionable spa. First known as The Prince's Theatre and later refurbished and renamed, it served the community as a civic theatre, giving room to touring companies and housing the local drama and operatic groups.

The old theatre was battered and shabby, but Beth loved it. The decorative carving in the auditorium and foyer was chipped and broken and everything needed a good dust and a coat of paint. But shabby as it was, and smelling as it did of fusty drapes and ancient scene-paint, Beth revelled in it all.

Pushing through the scene dock door she hurried down the passage heading for the stage. It was narrow with rooms leading off on either side. Immediately on the left was Mr Lamb's boiler room, which doubled as his office. Beth had never been inside Mr Lamb's sanctum.

He didn't encourage visitors. As far as she knew, none of her friends had passed the threshold. Sam had peeked through the keyhole once and Beth had seen him do it. She couldn't forget what had happened next, and each time she began the trip down the corridor the memory returned, unbidden.

It was coffee time and she had been about to leave the scene dock and go to the green room but paused when she caught sight of Sam through one of the glass panels of the swing doors. He was in the passage, bent double and squinting through the boiler-room keyhole.

Suddenly the boiler-room door had been pulled sharply inwards, tipping Sam off balance. As he struggled to right himself Mr Lamb stepped out.

"Why, look who's here!" he had said. "It's Runty Forrest. I thought it was MI5." He was a big meaty man who towered above Sam's slight figure.

Beth had watched helplessly through the glass as Mr Lamb stretched out a burly arm and picked Sam up by the front of his sweatshirt. He held him up until his face was on a level with his own. Then he walked a few steps with Sam hanging limply in his grasp and dropped him casually, like some sort of insect. With an unpleasant smirk he dusted his hands, turned on his heel and walked away.

Sam had stayed where he was dropped. Beth was horrified. She loathed violence of that sort and although she wanted to rush to Sam she held back. Some sixth sense had told her that he would hate to know anyone had seen his humiliation. He was the smallest of the boys in their group and fiercely sensitive about his height.

Then Jo had come from the green room end of the passage with a pile of old shirts over her arm and Sam had scrambled to his feet. That broke the spell for Beth and she had gone to join them.

Now, as she passed Lamb's door, she thought of him behind it, lurking like some gross spider, waiting until he could come out and gorge on people weaker than himself.

Pushing the thought away, she walked on.

Next to the boiler room were the washrooms and toilets and on the right two dressing rooms – one long room that could be divided into two if necessary and one "star" dressing room where the principals changed. At the end of the passage the green room spanned both sides of the space, making the shape of the head of a letter T. Off the green room lay the small costume room where Jo, in charge of all the SAPS' costumes, worked.

The actors could relax in the green room on the assortment of easy chairs, and brew up coffee as they waited for their cues on the stage above. They reached this by a flight of steps just outside the green room, leading directly into the wings. Anyone wanting to make an entrance from the other side of the stage had to walk behind the canvas cyclorama to get there.

As she struggled to open the green-room door Beth hoped the rehearsal had managed to go on without her props and that Sam was exaggerating as usual. She really didn't want to upset Paula at this stage of the production.

She pushed the door open with her foot and edged herself and loaded tray round it. Someone was in there, bending over the sink. There was a rush of water from the tap.

"Paula!" said Beth, surprised and a little breathless. "I'm on my way. I got waylaid with—" She stopped abruptly as Paula Barton swung round to face her.

"Are you OK?" Paula was preparing to take an aspirin. She looked pale.

"Beastly head." She put the aspirin in her mouth and took a gulp of water from the mug she was holding. "It feels like a percussion group. My fault," she added with a rueful grin. "I was out to dinner last night and we got home rather late."

Beth noted the 'we' and made a sympathetic

face. "Poor you. Shall I carry on with these?" She indicated her trayful.

"Yes, they're wanted. Rob's up there taking Act Two. Tell them I won't be long. I just need a moment." Rob was the assistant producer.

"Right." Beth turned to go, then paused. "While you're here, should I take the keys for tomorrow? You remember," she went on as Paula didn't react, "I'm coming in early to open up for the scenery crew and mark out the stage for Act Three."

"So you are. It's Sunday – I'd forgotten, and Mr L . . ."

"Doesn't come in," Beth finished her sentence as Paula had come to a stop. "And you can have a lie-in – for a bit, anyway."

Paula made an effort to smile. "You're a friend," she said. "Look, I want to take a breath of air and let that aspirin work so I'll go out through the scene dock and slip the keys in your basket. It's there, isn't it?"

"By the prop-gallery steps as usual. Great, Paula. See you in a bit."

As she negotiated the stairs to the stage Beth wondered, not for the first time, how it was that Paula Barton made her feel so 'in charge' and responsible. Since she had come to take over the group three years ago there had been a marked difference. SAPS had emerged from being a motley crowd of teenagers with little true commitment, to the team they now were. Every SAP understood where their strength lay and what their place in the group was. Paula always spoke to them as equals and they felt she was one of them. 'SAPS against the world!' was their watchword.

Beth put the bulky tray thankfully on the props table in her corner of the wings, known as the Prompt Corner because it was where the prompter always sat. Due to a quirk of the design of The Tree it also doubled as the stage manager's corner. Some long-gone architect had put the mechanism for raising the front curtain on the wrong side of the stage. Anyway, there was much more room to manoeuvre that side, so it was convenient to use it for both. This was where she presided as stage manager, giving the cues for lights, music, difficult entrances, and any noises off. From there she also raised the curtain and made sure that every actor had the properties they needed for each scene. One dreadful night Beth had let Romeo go on stage without his dagger and Juliet had had nothing to kill herself with. She'd nearly died of shame!

"At last!"

"Sorry, Rob. Got held up."

"Well, at least Toni can hold her proper mirror now. It'll stop her looking longingly for her book. Two weeks to go, Bella!" Rob, assistant director, addressed his leading lady. "Paula said she wanted all lines by this weekend. Take it from the top again. Steve, your kick-off. Beth, would you prompt?"

With a sigh Beth picked up her script and pulled her chair to the edge of the pool of light. She flipped the typed pages over to the start of Act Two. Antonia, playing Bella Gardoni, and Steve, her lover, took up their positions and began.

Rob Walker, a year older than most of the others, shook back his dark lock of hair and took up his position in the stalls with his feet on the back of the seat in front.

Beth couldn't help smiling a little. Fancies himself, does Rob, she thought. Her eye was caught by a movement in the row behind him. Fiona McLaren, new to SAPS for this production, sighed and rested her chin in her hands. She was gazing rapturously at the back of Rob's head.

Beth's amusement deepened. Come to think of it, he's not alone, her thoughts rolled on. That little Fiona's fallen badly by the look of it.

"Miss Bella," Steve was saying, "you sing divinely . . ." He stopped with an anguished look on his face and turned towards Beth. "Er . . . prompt, please."

Beth concentrated. "May I be so bold . . ." she fed him.

Paula came in quietly from the front of house and sat at the back of the stalls. She sometimes did this, or asked Rob to do so, to make sure that the actors' words could be heard at the back of the theatre.

Beth's mind kept wandering. She hated prompting – it was too slow and static for her. She never liked sitting on the sidelines. Acting on the stage was not for her, either. What she enjoyed was holding the threads of a production in her hands and controlling it smoothly, tucked behind in her corner. She knew she was good at it and took great pride in every detail, but sitting with the book and waiting for the actors to forget their lines really tried her patience.

Her restless eye watched Paula's pale face as she brushed some hair away from her forehead with a tired gesture. She didn't look very well and Beth felt sorry for her. She knew that *Bella* was a large and complicated production for SAPS, with quite a lot hanging on its success. It was no wonder that Paula, who carried all the responsibility, should get the odd headache.

This brought her round to thinking about Toby's father, Robert Harris. He was a town councillor who loved The Tree and had devoted both time and his own money to the old place. He had been mainly responsible for hiring Paula, and most of the SAPS knew that they had begun to see a lot of each other.

Had Paula been with Toby's father last night? Beth thought it likely. She wondered what Toby would feel if they married. She quite liked the idea of Paula as a stepmother herself. Toby, on the other hand, had been a bit odd when a group of them had been teasing him about it. Why? His mother had been dead for so long now that it couldn't be that.

That was the cue for her to think of Toby. She got a warm feeling whenever she did. It was hard to remember when he began to be one of her circle. There was a time when she hadn't liked him very much – she had thought him to be spiky and a little sly. Looking at him now, tall, intelligent and well co-ordinated, it was hard to believe. They had got to know each other well in the past year. Of course they shared their deep love of theatre and devotion to The Tree. Toby had begun to take leads in the plays and to rely on Beth's ready help with his parts and she knew that if a job had to be done for the scenery, Toby would always be there. Without thinking deeply about it, she considered him her best friend – next, that is, to Jo, whom she had known since primary school.

Beth could tell that Rob was aware of Paula's presence at the back, because he took his feet off the seat in front and sat up rather straight.

"Beth!" His voice cut in. "Will you give Bella her line, please? Are you with us or not?"

"Sorry, um . . . is it, 'What can I say, my heart is beating so. . . ?'"

Antonia said impatiently, "It's halfway down the next page, Beth, after Cecil says 'The world will be at your feet.'"

"Fiona," said Rob, turning round to look at her, "take the book, will you? Beth's mind isn't on the job and we've lots to get through."

Fiona swept her cloud of dark hair from her face, hoping that Rob would be impressed by its lavish waves. She got eagerly to her feet and floated up the steps to the stage, holding out her hand for the script. Beth's surge of dislike caught her by surprise but she handed over the script with relief.

"You can sort out your own props for now," she called to them all. "Please put them back on the prop table when you've done." Thankfully, she headed towards the stairs.

"If you see Cheryl," Rob's voice followed her, "would you tell her she'll be on soon?"

"OK," Beth shouted back, thinking to herself that a word with Jo had to come before anything else.

Josephine Henly was sitting quietly sewing the hem of Bella Gardoni's evening cloak as Beth came through the green room and pushed open the costume-room door. It was just a cubby-hole really – large enough to hold a sewing-machine table, Jo's chair, a cupboard and several shelves, but not much else. A roomy store cupboard opened off it, housing items such as paint and brushes, paper and glue, boxes of threads, costume beads of all kinds and a medley of things deemed useful one day. The rails that held the finished costumes were kept in the dressing rooms or sometimes overflowed into the green room. The bulk of SAPS' costume collection had to be housed somewhere else. Piles of costumes waiting to be worked on lay around everywhere.

"Hi, Jo!"

Jo looked up and smiled. "How're things in the big world outside?" she asked.

Beth perched on a corner of the table, moving a top hat and a pair of spangled tights.

It must feel like another world in here, she thought to herself. Shut away with one tiny window, far away from all the bustle and excitement everywhere else. How does Jo stand it? She's in here for hours sometimes.

"Oh, you know," she said aloud.

"I can guess." Jo bent her head again and took another stitch.

Beth watched her with affection. Jo never seemed to hurry but the amount of work she got through was amazing. It had always been the same, even when they were at Tolford Primary together. Jo's copper head and Beth's light brown one would be bent over a joint project, Beth sucking her crayons and making very busy sounds while Jo, quiet as a mouse, always finished her side in half the time. Their friendship had never been shaken. Beth relied on Jo's steady support more than she realized.

"Rob's taking it just now – Paula's got a headache. He tried to get me to prompt. I escaped."

"Ah," said Jo, the corners of her eyes crinkling. She knew her Beth.

"Oh, I nearly forgot. The blood's ready if you need some for the cossies. Toby and Gary have done a lovely job."

"Fine." Jo sounded abstracted. She was struggling with a knot in her thread. "Blast!" she said as it broke.

Beth picked up the top hat and put it on her head. She stood up and looked in the mirror hanging above the cupboard.

"Me, d'you think?"

"Quite the stage-door Johnnie!" Jo gave up on her thread and spooled another length.

"Well, see you tomorrow, my little seamstress-in-the-cupboard. I must give Cheryl a call and be on my way. I promised to cook for Mum tonight – she's got a 'do' on."

Beth turned to put the top hat back on the table when she noticed a jamjar. It was full of Toby and Gary's stage blood.

"You've got some blood already!"

To her surprise Jo blushed. "Oh, yes I have. Silly

of me . . ." she tailed off. "I must have forgotten," she finished lamely.

Beth raised an eyebrow at her. "My friend has something to hide?" she asked roguishly. Jo grinned a little helplessly.

Beth knew better than to press her. If Jo didn't want to say anything then she wouldn't. It would be a waste of time trying. No one could be as silent as Jo if she had something she wanted to keep secret. But what could be secret about a jamjar of stage blood?

"When are you going to do the direful deed?"

"Oh . . ." Jo seemed to come back from a great distance. "When the costume's ready for it. I thought I'd better get some of the blood quickly before the boys start throwing it around in the duel scene. Metaphorically speaking," she added with a grin.

Beth felt reassured. Bella's costume in the last act would be duly drenched with her blood, so she could tick it off her list.

"OK, then I'll see you tomorrow. I'm getting here early to set things up. Just two weeks to go to opening. 'Bye!"

"'Bye, Beth!" Jo called after her. She put down her needle and stared hard at nothing for a long moment.

The light was on in the 'star' dressing room as Beth passed. She paused, wondering if she'd find

Cheryl there. Then a burst of laughter came from inside. She pushed the door open and four flushed faces turned to her, looking very slightly guilty.

"You're on stage soon, Cher," she said. Then she added, "What are you lot hiding, may I ask?"

Gary, Toby, Sam and Cheryl giggled.

"This," said Sam, holding out a piece of drawing paper.

It was a picture of a sheep in thick black felt-tip lines. The sheep's head was undeniably the face of Mr Lamb. Underneath the drawing was written in large capitals: A WOLF IN SHEEP'S CLOTHING. It was very good.

"Clever, isn't she?" said Toby, giving Cheryl a pat on the head. She giggled again and bit the end of the pen. Her face was still unnaturally flushed.

"What on earth are you going to do with this?" asked Beth. "He'll go mad if he sees it."

"We have every intention of getting him to see it." Gary's voice was grim and Cheryl's giggle hit a high note and stayed there.

Beth began to feel anxious. She wished the boys wouldn't egg Cheryl on like this. She didn't like the look of her at all.

"But," she urged, "he'll only make trouble . . ."

"Then he'll have to make trouble," said Toby.

"Not half as much trouble as we mean to make for him!" Sam was almost crowing. "Revenge is sweet!" And laughter shook them.

"Go *now*, Cher!" Beth broke in crisply. "Paula's got a headache and Rob's taking the rehearsal. Just go." She looked at the others, exasperation getting the better of her nerves. "I hope you know what you're doing."

Cheryl whipped the drawing out of Sam's fingers, slipped past Beth through the dressing-room door, blew the boys a kiss, and was gone. Her giggle floated after her.

"Never fear, nemesis is near," said Gary, and the boys began to laugh again.

Irritated beyond words, Beth left them to it. "Just so long as they don't mess up the production . . ." she muttered.

She was nearing Mr Lamb's boiler room when she heard his radio switch off abruptly. Tinny laughter from a comedy programme was left hanging in mid-air. His door opened. He came out and shut it behind him. Beth found that he was standing in her way. She paused, unsure how to get round him. You never knew with Baa-Baa – he enjoyed being obstructive.

He was a big man whose florid good looks were going fast. Whatever charm he might have had was being eroded by his slack mouth and softening stomach. He wore his regulation overalls over a none-too-clean T-shirt, favouring the macho look he thought it gave him, and a lock of greasy hair was combed to fall over one eye in a sexy manner.

The SAPS sent him up unmercifully behind his back. Sam (it *would* be Sam) could take him off perfectly. Baa-Baa knew this and hated Sam for it. He harassed him whenever he came upon him alone. He'd pull his ears, twist his arms or trip him up at every opportunity. Baa-Baa had learned bully-boy tactics from his mother's knee.

"Why!" he said, watching Beth's hesitation with satisfaction. "If it isn't little Miss Tree herself. Don't tell me you're going home so soon?"

Beth opened her mouth to ask him to move but he didn't give her the chance.

"Mind you," he sniggered, "there's precious little mys-tery about you, is there?" He sniggered again, pleased with his pun.

What a slob, Beth thought. He looks drunk. She made herself look him in the eye.

"May I pass, please?"

Lamb took a step towards her. Beth could smell his beery breath. She stepped back. Baa-Baa grinned and took another step towards her. He was in his element.

"Why don't you do something about yourself?" he leered at her. "Take some lessons from your sexy friend. She could teach you a thing or two." He ran his tongue round his lips obscenely.

Beth, stepping back again in spite of herself, could feel the power of the man. It took her by surprise. A stab of genuine fear ran through her.

"Yeah," he reached out a hand. It was dirty, with black under the fingernails. "Fix your hair, get yourself some real clothes, know what I mean?"

To her horror she found she was frozen to the spot. Her helplessness added to his pleasure, and she could see him relish it. God! she thought. He's not a spider, he's a snake – and I'm his rabbit!

"Everything OK, Beth?"

Toby was coming through the green-room door. He had seen the way Lamb was looking at her.

"Toby!" His name came out in a breath. Beth never thought she'd be so glad to see anyone.

Baa-Baa backed off fast and retreated to his door. He went in and shut it behind him with a slam.

The rest of her breath came out in a jerk.

"What's up? What's the pig been saying to you?" Toby was glaring at the boiler-room door as if he'd like to smash it down.

Beth wanted to lean against him, her legs were so wobbly with relief, but there was no way she could repeat Baa-Baa's foul innuendoes to Toby. So she managed to shrug and say, her voice almost steady, "One of Baa-Baa's stupid jokes. He really is the pits!"

"It looked like more than a joke to me, Beth." Toby's face changed and he went on quietly, "Never mind. He'll be laughing on the other side of his face tonight."

Alarmed, Beth saw the dangerous line of his mouth was back.

"If he lays a finger on you, you tell me, you hear? I'll . . ."

The rush of warm feeling Beth felt as she saw Toby's concerned face helped to calm her.

"Really, it wasn't very much," she said quickly. "Really." She could see he didn't want to believe her and her unease over the plot the boys had been hatching got the better of her.

"He was being difficult about the keys for the paint cupboard tomorrow – you know what he's like," she lied. "He just loves his power." And she watched, with relief, as Toby's face relaxed a little.

"Well," he said, "glad I came by, anyway. You off now?"

Beth nodded. "I'm just getting my basket. See you tomorrow, Galahad!" She wanted to say, "Just leave it. Don't mix it with Lamb – he's dangerous," but it seemed an over-reaction so she tried a cheery smile and fell back on the old theatrical blessing.

"Break a leg, will you!"

Toby grinned wolfishly and disappeared into the men's washroom.

Beth had never been pestered by Lamb in that kind of way before. He usually went for the obviously pretty SAPS, and just used his position to obstruct her whenever he could, withholding

Beth hoped she would see her one day. It would bring her closer to her greatest longing, which was to have known the theatre in its heyday. How she wished she could have seen the then Prince's Theatre when it was brand new, all gilded and beautiful and full of ladies and gentlemen scented and bewigged, watching the fashionable actors of the day strutting and declaiming on the very stage that SAPS were using now. Each time she thought of that it made her feel a little dizzy.

She unlocked her bike and, strapping her basket firmly to the back, began to pedal home.

3

Sunday morning. It was the sort of July day that begins bright but clouds over by lunchtime and ends in rain.

Beth leaned on her bedroom window sill and felt the warmth of the early sun. She lived with her mother in a small terraced house on the edge of Tolford Regis. Her parents had agreed to split three years ago and her father had gone to live closer to his work, about eighty kilometres away. He had a new wife now, but Beth saw as much of him as they could manage. Her mother didn't bear him a grudge. She had a job in a large chemist's in the High Street and plenty of friends. The little 'do' last night was for a group of them. It had been a success, Beth remembered happily. The orange and chicken casserole, smothered in toasted almonds, had gone down very well.

She stretched and yawned and headed for the bathroom, thinking with pleasure of the day ahead. Then she pulled on her black jeans and an old blue sweatshirt, her 'theatre gear' as she called it. She wore it for every production. It was part of her ritual, part of her personal superstition that dressing in the old familiar garments would somehow keep disasters at bay. Or perhaps, she thought, grinning wryly at herself, I'm just putting on my costume like everybody else.

Beth never gave much thought to the way she looked. When she did, however, it was with a sense of mild disapproval. Her face was oval without much colour and her fine brown hair fell in two wings on either side of it. Her nose was straight but she thought her mouth far too wide. What she couldn't see was the humour that made that wide mouth mobile and attractive, nor could she watch her expressions move behind the eyes that she considered dull. She put her tongue out at her face in the mirror and went past it to the door.

Downstairs Beth set about getting breakfast. Her mother was still asleep and she wanted her to stay that way. They had a good understanding and their life together was relaxed and undemanding. Her mother worried sometimes, with her divorce coming when Beth was only fourteen, that her daughter had been forced to grow up too fast and had lost out on a chunk of her early adolescence. This never occurred to Beth. She liked her life. She liked the freedom that living alone with her mother gave her.

At half past eight she was on her bike.

"I'll have the place all to myself for nearly an hour before the others arrive, if I can get there by nine," she thought and felt the tide of excitement begin to rise.

There was something so special about being the first into The Tree, entering the thick atmosphere alone and bringing it all to life by switching on the lights. The thought of Bella's ghost never bothered her. She half hoped she might find her sitting in the stalls absorbed by some unseen rehearsal, or surprise her as she put the last touches to her make-up in the star dressing room. Sometimes Beth could feel herself almost within touching distance of long-gone productions.

I'd never hear the end of it if the gang knew how I felt, she grinned to herself. Paula might understand, and Jo . . . and maybe Toby? Well, I'm not going to give them the chance to find out. I'm good old reliable and totally unimaginative Beth! She turned her bike into the car park and headed for her railing.

Fishing the theatre keys out of her basket she

fumbled for the lock. The door was unlocked. She stood back in surprise. Was Mr Lamb in? It was strange if he was. He made a point of never doing any overtime.

The theatre was in darkness. Light flooded the scene dock as Beth touched the switch and went to drop her basket in its usual spot by the prop-gallery steps. She listened but everything was quiet. Shrugging her shoulders she pulled out a sheet of paper and attached it to the scene dock wall with sticky tape. It was a list of things to be done for the gang of SAPS who had volunteered to build and paint the rather elaborate scenery for *Bella*. They were due in any time after ten o'clock.

Beth looked around, but there was nothing out of place. Burglars? Well, they'd be gone by now and what was done was done.

She armed herself with three reels of different coloured masking tape and set off for the stage. Each act of the play had to have its furniture and entrances marked out on the floor with a different coloured tape. This helped the stage staff to know exactly where to put the furniture and also helped the actors to learn their moves more precisely.

Beth went through the passage to the green room, switching on the lights. Nothing was out of place but there was a rather marked smell as she passed through it.

Some perfume, she thought, to hang about all

night! Perhaps it's the new stuff Jo's using for cleaning make-up off collars.

Gathering speed, she ran up the last steps onto the stage two at a time. The switch for the two great working spots was on a brick pillar just below the lighting gallery. It always made a most satisfying click when it was turned on or off. It did so today.

Light, white and harsh, flooded the area.

Nothing prepared Beth for what she saw.

Her feet were standing in a pool of red.

Within centimetres of her shoe, also lying in the red pool, was the body of a man. He lay completely still with both arms outstretched and his head turned away from her. He seemed to be red all over.

Then Beth saw the bucket. That too was lying on its side. It was the boys' blood bucket, now quite empty.

George Lamb, Baa-Baa, caretaker, was dead as mutton.

"Oh, God!" Beth whispered. Her horrified eyes stared at a piece of spattered paper clutched in one of the dead man's hands. She recognized the thick black lines – Cheryl's drawing.

"Oh, God!" she whispered again, unable to think.

The reels of masking tape dropped from her hands into the red tide one by one. She didn't notice.

"Oh . . . God . . ." With a great effort she commanded her legs to move and began to back away. The world had gone into slow motion. All noises ceased and in a shell of shock she forced herself away from the horror on the floor. Her trainers made red footprints on the stage, which faded as she trod the paint off. Was it only red paint on her shoes? Her mind froze again at the thought of what else it might be – and suddenly she was in the foyer of The Tree, clutching the pay phone and trying to push the buttons for 999 with a trembling finger.

"Which service?" The faraway voice sounded cool and remote.

Beth didn't know. "I'm at The Tree," she stammered. "There's someone dead – I think he's dead – he's not moving . . ."

"What's your name, caller? Where are you now?" The voice didn't seem to understand.

"My name's Beth Greene." She suddenly felt sick. "I'm at The Tree Theatre . . . please send someone . . . please . . ." She dropped the phone and sat down abruptly, hanging her head between her knees. She didn't hear the voice on the other end of the phone say, "All right, dear. Just hold on – we'll get someone to you."

Slowly the dreadful nausea subsided along with the numbness in her mind and body, and she knew where she was and what she had seen. As she slowly replaced the phone, wondering how long it would take for the emergency services to arrive, another thought came.

"The gang! They'll be here soon. They'll come looking for me – they mustn't see . . . I've got to warn them."

She couldn't go back the way she had come. She'd have to pass . . . she couldn't do it. She'd go out the front of the theatre and walk behind to the scene dock door and stay there until somebody came.

So she struggled with the bolts of The Tree's heavy glass door and walked into the noise of Tolford Regis's busy High Street until she could turn the corner of the theatre, cross to the stage-door steps, and sit and wait for someone to arrive.

4

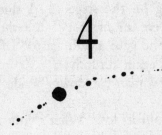

Beth tensed as she saw the police car turn in to The Tree's car park and her feeling of unreality deepened. Countless television plays had this scene in them, but this wasn't television. She felt vulnerable and alone as she watched the two police officers get out and walk towards her. She stood up slowly.

"Good morning." One of the policemen, a tall young man with ginger hair and freckles, smiled at her. "You've got trouble?"

They were both quite young. The other was a woman police officer with her blonde hair tucked into her hat. She smiled too and they both waited for Beth to speak.

She took a deep breath.

"I think our caretaker's dead," she heard herself say clearly and slowly.

"Dead? You mean Mr Lamb?"

Beth frowned. Did he know him? She nodded.

"What makes you think he's dead?"

"He's lying on the stage . . . I think he must have been there all night . . . the theatre wasn't locked . . ." She gave a little gasp. "I found him." She sat down again abruptly.

The policewoman sat down beside her on the steps.

"Tell us about it, love. What's your name?" she asked gently.

Beth, feeling glad of her nearness, told her.

"I got here early. We've a production going, you see. I had things to do. Paula – Mrs Barton – let me have the keys. Mr Lamb doesn't come in on Sundays . . . and . . . I . . ." her voice tailed off. She couldn't bring herself to go any further.

"On the stage, you say?" The policeman stepped in to help. "Don't worry, I'll go take a look. I know the way." He suddenly grinned. "I was a SAP myself once, you know. That's how I know Mr Lamb."

Beth blinked. Policemen and SAPS didn't equate somehow.

He saw her surprise and smiled. "You know the old saying, 'Once a SAP always a SAP'?" He raised his eyebrows and waited for her response. She smiled shakily as they spoke the words together, "In more ways than one!"

"You'll have to go in through the scene dock," she told him, relieved to think he knew his way about The Tree. "The stage door is still locked."

He patted her shoulder lightly and went.

Toby walked into view. His house was not far away. Beth saw his carefree saunter freeze as he registered the police car. She was so pleased to see him that it took her by surprise. His tall figure with its thatch of straw-coloured hair was so familiar and so comforting, somehow.

"Toby!" she called, leaving the policewoman sitting on the steps and taking a few paces towards him.

"Hi, Beth! What have you been up to?"

"Mr Lamb's had an – accident . . ." Toby's face went stiff. Beth watched his eyes narrow a little.

"Good show," he said in his best Noel Coward voice.

"He's dead, Toby."

"Say again."

Beth wanted to shake him. Why wouldn't he understand? She suddenly felt angry.

"He's lying on the stage, covered in your beastly blood, and dead as a doornail!" She stopped, horrified at herself as the blood drained slowly out of Toby's face.

"Oh God, Toby! I'm so sorry! I found him, you see . . ."

They stood staring at each other for what seemed ages and then the policeman returned. His freckles were standing out clearly on his white face and he was tucking his radio back into its sheath.

"I've alerted the station," he said quietly to his colleague, who had been watching Beth and Toby from the steps. "He's dead all right. It's a CID job. There's one hell of a mess up there."

Coming up to Beth he nodded to Toby and said, "I need Mrs Barton's phone number – she's got to be informed. Beth, the CID officers will want your statement. They'll want to question anyone involved with The Tree so, when the rest of the group turn up they'd better stay put for a bit."

Toby asked suddenly, "How'd he die? What killed him?"

"Hard to say right now," the policeman replied. "He's covered in some sort of paint. Could be a blow on the head, but we'll have to wait for forensic. You're a SAP, I take it, sir?"

"Toby Harris."

"Councillor Harris's son?"

Toby nodded, white-faced.

"The Tree's got a lot to thank your dad for, then," he said kindly. "I was a member when he had the old stage repaired and fixed the washrooms. Didn't half make a difference to the life of a SAP."

"Yeah," said Toby, as from a far distance. "He's a theatre fan, my dad."

"Well, I'm going to leave you with my colleague, PC Collins here. Why not take her into the theatre and make some coffee till the others arrive?" He looked at their white faces.

"It's a terrible thing to have happened, I know. Look, it'll get sorted out once the big guns get here. Don't worry. Just tell the truth and it'll all come out right. You'll see," he said reassuringly as he climbed into the police car and drove away.

"Right, you two," PC Collins straightened up. "Where's that coffee, then?"

Conquering her feeling of dread at the thought of returning to the silent theatre, Beth led the way back into The Tree with Toby following behind, pale and grim.

Several SAPS had gathered by the time Paula appeared in the green room. They were clutching their mugs of coffee rather like drowning people were supposed to clutch at straws. An unusual hush lay over the room. People lowered their voices and some even whispered. Everyone was conscious that George Lamb was lying dead on the stage upstairs.

Two CID officers had arrived, a sergeant and a detective inspector. The forensic team had come soon after and so had a police photographer. They were all on the stage.

Beth sipped her coffee, huddled in a corner.

Shock had made her cold and shivery. Jo, one of the first to get there after Toby, was in the costume room sorting out a wrap to put over Beth's shoulders. She was quietly taking care of her. Jo had said very little. She hugged Beth for a moment and then went and put her things away. Her face was very white and had a shut, thoughtful look. It was impossible to guess what she was feeling. Beth remembered seeing the same closed look – was it only yesterday? – when she saw the jamjar of blood on her sewing table. Her mind skittered back to the scene dock plotting and Cheryl's clever drawing. They all hated Mr Lamb, but surely . . .

"Oh, what a mess," she sighed and scanned the room for her friends. She saw, with slight surprise, that Gary and Sam were sitting side by side against one wall intent on watching Toby. He was on the edge of a group of people in the centre of the green room, talking earnestly to Cheryl, whose large blue eyes were glued to his face as if her life depended on it. After their anti-Lamb demonstrations yesterday Beth thought they'd all be together, probably gloating. Her eyes lingered for a second on Toby's tall figure bending a little over Cheryl's and noticed how her fingers plucked at his sleeve as she listened to him.

Little minx, said her inner voice. Wasn't Gary enough for you? Everyone knew she'd been knocking about with him all through the last production. But, her inner voice told her, Toby had more sense than to be taken in by all that little-girl-take-care-of-me stuff. She pulled her gaze away and noticed, with a flicker of humour, that Rob was standing with one arm around Fiona's shoulders and she was leaning on him for support. She's another Cheryl, Beth observed wryly. They don't miss a trick.

Paula's entrance broke in on her thoughts.

"Beth!" Paula came up to her. "What on earth's going on?"

"Haven't the police told you?" Surely she knew.

"It's really true, then? He's dead?" She read Beth's face. "How?"

"They don't know yet."

"I must go up – I must see—" She turned quickly.

"Paula, you can't. They're all up there." But Paula was halfway to the door.

It opened. Detective Chief Inspector Armitage stood in the doorway. He had entered The Tree by the front doors and none of the group in the green room had seen him arrive.

He was a burly man in his early fifties with thinning hair going grey at the temples. The green-room lights bounced off the lenses of his metal-rimmed glasses, giving him a rather blind, slightly sinister look. His cheeks were pale and fleshy with heavy lines from nose to chin. Beth was suddenly reminded of a blind old dog. She shivered.

Silence fell in the green room.

"Good morning, everyone!" His voice held authority but was not unpleasant as he introduced himself.

"I'm sorry to have penned you all in here," he went on. "You'll understand, I'm sure, that there's a great deal to do in a case like this."

Silence.

He went on. "Everyone here knows by now that Mr Lamb, the caretaker of this theatre, is dead. The circumstances of his death are, to say the least, suspicious. We now know that he died sometime around ten o'clock on Saturday night, that is, yesterday. About that time some person or persons as yet unknown dropped a bucket of red paint on his head. The bucket also contained a heavy stage weight. It killed him outright. We are treating his death as murder."

Around ten o'clock? Beth struggled to think. That must have been about the time the rehearsal finished.

No one moved. He noticed Paula.

"Mrs Barton?" Paula nodded, unable to trust her voice to be steady.

"Good. Now, we'll want to question everyone here and then you'll be free to go home. Mrs Barton, perhaps you'd arrange somewhere for us to use as an interview room? And I'd like a list of anybody connected with the theatre or anyone who knew Mr Lamb and might be able to help us."

"One of you boys," Paula said a little huskily, "put a folding table in the star dressing room for the Chief Inspector. There are chairs in there already. Will that be all right?"

"Splendid. Now, I wonder . . ." Armitage paused and the room waited. "I wonder if anyone knows anything about this?"

With a rather dramatic gesture he held a piece of paper above his head. It was spattered with red marks that looked like blood, but everybody could clearly read the title, A WOLF IN SHEEP'S CLOTHING, sprawling across it in large black capitals.

Quietly for her, and without fuss, Cheryl fainted.

Beth watched them gather round the fallen girl.

"Oh God, this is all awful!" she thought, as she remembered where she had last seen the drawing, clenched in Mr Lamb's still hand.

Consciousness returned to Cheryl and she began to cry. Paula wanted her carried into the large dressing room.

"I'll stay with her," Toby stepped forward almost too quickly and Paula gave him a grateful look. A shaky Cheryl reached for his hand. Beth's stomach tightened.

The thought that she might be getting jealous of Cheryl came as a shock. She knew how she felt about Toby, or she thought she did. They were a good team. She knew he valued her and enjoyed her company and she his. She never had to pretend with him, never had to flirt and resort to little female tricks. She wouldn't have known how anyway. They had laughed at others together and she believed that was how it would be. But now, watching Cheryl, she knew she couldn't compete – not on that ground, if that was what Toby wanted. But why did she care? Did she feel more than friendship for him? Or was it just because she couldn't bear to play second-best to Cheryl's first?

It was all too complicated, she decided. This was certainly not the time for self-searching, not when there were other more desperate questions to be answered.

5

Paula Barton was the first to go into the star dressing room to be questioned. She was in there about fifteen long minutes. She was the Creative Administrator of The Tree so she could give the police a valuable overview of the people who came into contact with Mr Lamb. She could also furnish them with the names and addresses of SAP members.

The SAP members present sat in virtual silence.

"They want you next, Beth," Paula said, emerging at last. She had lines around her mouth, Beth noticed, that hadn't been there before, but she managed a smile.

The star dressing room looked the same as it always did. The long striplights above the big make-up mirrors were on and made the three policemen in the room look strangely overlit and theatrical. DCI Armitage sat behind a flimsy folding card table. He looked as if he would take it with him if he stood up. His legs stuck out beyond it. There was nowhere else for them to go. Another policeman sat near him with a notebook on his knee and PC Collins stood at ease next to the door. For all the incongruity of the scene, Beth's taut nerves stretched even further.

"You are Beth Greene?" DCI Armitage spoke quietly, and Beth nodded.

"Sit down, Beth." He indicated the chair in front of his table. Beth sat.

"Now," he began kindly, "tell me exactly what you did this morning when you came into the theatre."

So she did, as calmly as she could.

"The theatre door was not locked, you say? Were you surprised?"

"Yes. It's the last thing Mr Lamb always does. It's always the scene dock door."

"About this bucket of paint – or blood." Beth tensed. "D'you know who mixed it?"

Anxiety gripped Beth and she said, "I think some of the boys did."

"Who exactly?" Armitage seemed prepared to dig away.

"I . . . I'm not sure . . ." Armitage raised his eyebrows. Beth knew she wasn't a good liar. It wasn't something she ever did. She knew she was going red.

"I'm going to have to ask them all, Beth. It would save a lot of time."

"Toby Harris and Gary Smith," she said with a sinking feeling in her stomach.

"Making the blood doesn't mean they did anything with it, you know," Armitage said gently, seeing her distress. "Now, when was the last time you saw it?"

That was easier. "Just after they finished making it. Then I had to go on stage."

"Time?"

Beth thought. "About five o'clock."

"And this drawing," he pointed to it as it lay in front of him on the green felt top of the table. "Did you ever see it before this morning?"

Cheryl's white, unconscious face settled it for Beth. "No, I haven't." Done it now, she thought.

"Have you any idea why it should have been in Mr Lamb's hand?"

"None at all." Absolutely none.

"Thank you, Beth," DCI Armitage said. "If you think of anything else that might help us you know where to find us, don't you?"

Beth nodded and stood up gratefully.

"Mrs Barton told me," Armitage said as PC Collins was about to open the door, "that you were someone of great integrity. I'm sure she's right."

Beth stumbled out of the star dressing room in a blur. Her confusion and distress brought a return of the numbness she had experienced when she first saw Mr Lamb's dead body. Thinking was out of the question. Why had she lied about the drawing? What had her friends been up to? Everything seemed a step too far to go.

Think . . . I must have time to think . . . She evaded the questioning eyes around her and returned to her seat next to Jo.

One by one the SAPS went into the star dressing room. They came out again, subdued and more than a little frightened. Detective Chief Inspector Armitage was gentle with them, as he had been with Beth, but the violent and mysterious death of the caretaker had shaken them. More than ever they needed each other. They needed to talk themselves back into some semblance of the world they knew. Most of them, however, went home to tell their parents, await developments, and find out what all this would mean for SAPS.

Jo took Cheryl home in a taxi. Beth, Sam and Gary found themselves biking slowly round to Toby's house. Toby walked with them. Paula had been the last to leave the Tree so no-one knew where she went. She'd phone them all, she said, and let them know when – and if – SAPS would be meeting again.

Nobody said very much. They moved along in a tight group, each wrapped in their own bleak thoughts. True to its promise the weather had clouded over before midday and now heavy clouds hurried before a warm west wind. Rain wasn't far away.

Toby's house was in the once fashionable part of Tolford Regis. It was a handsome stone house with a Georgian façade, not far from The Tree. Mr Harris was a very busy man, with many irons in the fire, so he was often out. Groups of Toby's friends took to gathering there after school or at weekends. It had become a habit.

Only when they were sitting in Toby's familiar kitchen and clutching cold drinks from the fridge did any of them manage to speak.

"I wonder if your dad knows yet?" Beth asked Toby.

"He's in a meeting all day," Toby replied. "Perhaps Paula's managed to get to him. He'll space out."

There was a pause. It was common knowledge that Mr Harris and Paula were more than good friends but no one said much about it, at least not to Toby. Eight years ago his mother had died in a road accident. Toby's father had been driving and had got through with little damage, but Toby had taken a long time to forgive his father. Sometimes he thought he never would, even now, forget who had been responsible for killing his mother. They never talked about it, they never mentioned her, and they never got close to each other.

Toby's father had a thriving business distributing groceries. He worked hard for his success and Toby was looked after when he lost his mother by a series of after-school minders and his friends' parents. Loss and neglect had made their mark on him in those early days. Mr Harris's own guilt made it difficult for him to face his son and when Toby began to get into trouble of one sort or another he could only react harshly. In the last two years Toby had grown enormously fast, almost outstripping his father. He had kept out of trouble and a kind of truce now existed between them. At least they shared their feelings and interest in The Tree and his father could be proud of Toby's emerging acting talent.

So, of course, could Paula Barton, as she had encouraged him when she saw his potential. She had given him parts that stretched his ability and under her charge Toby had blossomed. Paula, with her aura of glamour and quiet authority was such fun to be with. Toby badly needed her good opinion, as much as he still dreaded and feared his father's bad one. She acted as a kind of bridge between them and soon both he and his father were completely under her spell.

At last Toby spoke, looking at Beth. "You didn't

tell them that it was Cheryl's drawing, did you?" he asked.

"No," she said, "I didn't." He's protecting her, she thought. But then, so had she. Cheryl seemed to have that knack.

"I hope Cheryl's going to be OK. I know what she's like," Gary said slowly.

"Oh, I think she will be. We had a bit of a talk." Toby sounded very certain and a little smug.

"Oh, naturally." Gary was stung. "You, of course, know her better than I do. She'll do anything you say!"

Toby didn't reply but turned his glass round on the table.

"What do you mean, 'a bit of a talk'?" Beth cut in quickly before Toby was forced to clarify his position with Cheryl. The last thing they wanted at this point was a row over her, she thought grimly. "The girl fainted. Talking's not going to help her much."

"I mean," said Toby deliberately, "I managed to calm her down." It sounded as if he meant something other than that.

"Good," said Sam flatly.

"What d'you mean, 'good'?" Beth asked. None of this sounded right to her.

"Hey," said Sam brightly, "did you see old Rob and that little Fiona?"

"Don't change the subject, Sam," said Beth. She

put her elbows on the table and tried to fix them all with her eyes. It wasn't easy. No one was looking at her.

"Look," she said as firmly as she could. "Look, it's me, Beth, your chum, mate, whatever. I'm not Chief Inspector Whatsisname. Don't forget, I know you lot. I heard you plotting something yesterday, something to do with that blood you made and Cheryl's drawing, heaven knows what. So tell me, what did you do? What are you all hiding?"

The boys looked at each other.

"Nothing," said Toby, staring at the table.

"Nothing, honest, Bethikins," said Sam, almost jauntily.

"Gary?" Beth looked at him.

"No, Beth, nothing." His glasses had slipped down his nose and he sounded miserable.

Beth sighed and stood up.

"I'm off home," she said. "Mum won't believe it – rehearsal night and all. I don't believe it myself, none of it."

"I'll come." Gary pushed his chair back. He lived further on from Beth's house and they often biked back together after late evenings at The Tree.

Although it was only afternoon it felt like a week to Beth since she had set off in the sunshine that Sunday morning. As they pedalled along side by side she was struggling with guilty feelings of her own. She hadn't told the Detective Chief Inspector that she knew who had done the drawing found in Mr Lamb's hand. She had said she knew nothing about it. It seemed impossible to tell him it was Cheryl's work when she was clearly so unnerved. She doubted if anybody else had told him and she needed time to think. Was that what the boys were all being so funny about? Mr Lamb wasn't killed by a savage drawing. It had to be something more than that.

At Beth's front gate Gary paused as she fumbled with the latch. She sensed he wanted to say something more.

"'Bye, Gary."

"Beth . . ."

"Yes?" She waited.

"I . . . just . . . think you're great. 'Bye," he blurted and pedalled swiftly away.

That's not what he really wanted to say, Beth thought as she put her bike in the garden shed, wishing that she had tried to pin him down while she had the chance. Still, if he means it, it's sweet of him. She had a soft spot for Gary. She admired his cleverness and vitality and it was always nice to be liked. Even though she felt that he really wanted to tell her something else and had said what he did to cover his confusion she didn't mind. He was a good friend. She didn't really want him to get closer to her than the others in her circle and she certainly didn't want to follow in Cheryl's shoes, but he was good to have around. Unlike Sam he never went too far . . . well, not often. Sam always did. Whatever joke, whatever prank, even whatever anger gripped him, Sam's self-control was minimal.

But there was nothing to say that Sam had played a leading role in whatever the others had done. He had been a latecomer to the plot. She sighed as she saw once again Toby's grim face, Cheryl's glittering hate, Gary's kicked bucket crashing against the scene dock wall and Sam's unholy glee at it all.

Oh, Gary! she wondered suddenly. It's not just Sam this time. Have you all gone too far?

As if on cue, there was a clap of thunder and drops of rain as big as peanuts began to fall.

Beth rushed for the back porch and let herself into the kitchen. The familiar look of it filled her with gratitude. The warm smell of it wrapped around her and the stress of the day took a step back. Her mother was at home – she could hear her moving about upstairs. Beth didn't know what time of day it was or anything. Around teatime, she thought – she couldn't remember lunchtime. She felt unbearably tired and tears of exhaustion began to prick her eyes as she went into the hall, dropping her basket at the foot of the stairs.

"I'm back, Mum!" she called.

Her mother's voice, surprised and pleased,

answered her. "Already, love? Is everything all right?"

Hearing her mother's voice, loving and concerned, was too much for Beth. She sat down on the bottom stair, put her head in her hands and cried as if she was six years old.

6

"You know, Jo," Beth said slowly, "it's rather like being suspended in . . ." she searched for the right word, ". . . jelly."

"What is?" Jo was lying on her back under an apple tree. She sounded far away.

"Well, all this." Beth, propped up on an elbow, waved an arm.

Jo sat up and looked about her. She saw a dozen or so apple trees in full leaf, and a little way away, her home.

"Jelly?"

"Yes," said Beth. "Not here, idiot, but the situation we're all in. I haven't had a call from Paula yet, have you?"

Jo shook her head.

"Well, there you are – jelly. Can't move. Can't go up and can't go down. Stuck."

"She's probably up to her eyes in it. She looked dreadful yesterday. There's a lot to arrange, I expect." Jo tailed off vaguely. Beth knew she was equally anxious to know what was going to happen.

It seemed unbelievable that they could be lying in Jo's familiar orchard, talking together as they loved to do on any other long summer's day. The difference was that now death, like some dark finger, had touched them both and they didn't know where it would lead them.

After that initial clap of thunder the promised storm had followed and raged for most of the night. Wind and rain beat down the fields of corn and tossed flower petals all over the gardens. By morning, however, it had blown itself out. The day had come in clean and peaceful as if to make amends for the violence of the night. The sun glowed on the girls' faces and warmed the tiny green apples above them. Jo's Irish sheepdog, Ruffle, put a hard paw on Beth's leg. She was lying in between them and wanted attention. Beth stroked her absent-mindedly.

Far away in the old stone farmhouse the phone rang. The girls turned as one and stared towards the sound. Jo half rose to her feet. A face appeared at the kitchen window. Her mother hardly had to call her name when Jo was up and running towards the back door with Ruffle bounding after her.

Watching her long copper hair swinging behind her, Beth saw a damp patch on Jo's jeans where she had been lying, and getting to her feet she felt her own bottom. Damp too. But this hardly registered. A hard knot of anxiety formed in her stomach. It had to be Paula on the phone. She had said she'd get in touch with them all and maybe she'd tried and she'd left for Jo's before her call came through.

Beth had a strong and sudden premonition that this interlude in Jo's summer orchard, so normal and safe, was to be treasured. She had biked over to Jo's house like a mad thing after breakfast, arriving hot and sweaty. She had needed to be there, to talk things over with Jo, to try to lay the horror of the previous day to rest in the wholesome calm of that place and that family.

Jo would have laughed if anyone had suggested her home was a calm one. Her mother and father were both working potters. They had converted one of the old barns of the farmhouse into an efficient pottery where, with the help of one other potter, they produced a range of usable and attractive pottery which they sold to shops in the larger towns and around the country at craft fairs.

Jo had two sisters, one of fourteen and the baby, Beanie, who had made a sudden appearance three years ago. She was such a long thin baby that her father had said she was made like a runner. Her real name was Elizabeth. Ruffle, friendly and silly, rubbed along with two cats and a hutch full of flopeared rabbits.

They were always in the throes of some real-life drama there. Jo's father, wild-bearded and erratic, created eddies of energy as he passed by and Pat, his wife, sailed through them with humour and a wonderful acceptance. This warm acceptance was like a tablecloth spread on a huge table, seating anyone who came to it. Jo, unlike her sturdy little mother to look at, had inherited much of this characteristic and Beth was attracted to it like a magnet.

All this sanity she thought, drinking it in, and I've lied to the police about a murder! It's like a nightmare. Why can't I wake up?

Jo appeared at the kitchen door as Beth came up to her.

"Good news or bad news first?" she asked, not smiling.

"Good," said Beth, in need of it.

"*Bella* goes on, but . . ." she said as she saw Beth's relieved face, "not until the Lamb's buried on Thursday. The theatre's shut till then, in respect for him."

What respect? thought Beth, but she still didn't like to say what everyone felt – that Mr Lamb had commanded very little liking, let alone respect.

"Lunch, girls," Pat Henly's voice came from the kitchen.

"We're going to see how Cheryl is after lunch, Mum," Jo said as they took their places round the large pine table. Beanie was already there, tucking into a plate of egg fingers and tomatoes.

"Dreadful, dreadful business," her mother said as she put a bowl of salad in front of them, followed by a wooden board full of cheese and slices of ham. "Eat up, dears. I'm taking some sandwiches out to the workshop – got a full kiln to load. Beanie, you come on out when you've had enough, OK?"

Beanie nodded with her mouth full.

"Bread's in the bin, and you know where the butter is," Pat's voice floated at them through the door. She was on her way. She came back for a second. "Help yourselves to fruit," she added.

But the girls were not very hungry. They ate what they could, stacked the dishes and put the food away as soon as little Beanie was finished. Then, shouting their goodbyes through the pottery door, they began to bike the journey to town.

Jo's home was about three kilometres south of Tolford Regis. Beth had to bike through the centre of town to get to it as her home was on the northern edge just before the houses and shops gave way to the green hills of Dorset.

They entered the town close to the railway

station, not far from Sam's flat. This was now the industrial part of town carrying a few light industries and a major cheese factory. It was not considered to be as good a part to live in as north Tolford, on the other side of the river Tol, where The Tree was and where Toby and Gary lived. Cheryl's semi-detached house was on the south bank of the river. The group of respectable villas had been built after the Second World War and gave the impression of having drawn themselves apart from the rough and tumble of the rest of the area.

Cheryl's mother opened the door. She was a large, motherly woman who always dressed in a jumper and skirt no matter what time of year it was. The jumpers were short-sleeved in summer and the skirts fuller, but the look was the same. She smiled at the girls on her doorstep.

"In you come, dears," she said. "Cheryl will be pleased to see you. She's in there." She indicated the sitting-room door.

"Who's that?" Mr King's voice came from his study upstairs. He stepped onto the landing, pen in hand, and looked relieved when he saw Jo and Beth.

"Thank the Lord," he said, "no more reporters." He retreated into his study again.

"Reporters?" Jo and Beth asked together. They hadn't thought of reporters.

"I left home early," Beth said, relieved to think she'd escaped. "And Jo lives further out. I suppose they'd try the nearby SAPS first."

Mrs King sighed. "Pests! They were waiting for Cheryl after church, and the phone keeps on ringing. Cheryl's so upset."

Beth realized how troubled she looked. Her kindly, plain face was clearly very anxious. "As if our Cheryl could tell them anything! She's so upset. You must all be upset," she added, looking at them for the first time. "It's so hard to know what to think – and the police . . ."

"Police again?" Beth asked sharply. "Have they found out anything more?"

"I don't think so, dear," Mrs King replied. "Cheryl said they just asked the same questions over again. I suppose they have to do their job. Anyway, go on in to her. I'll bring you a cup of tea."

She turned back to the open kitchen door. As Beth was about to reach for the sitting-room door handle she caught a glimpse of a woman sitting at the kitchen table. Her eyes were red with weeping and Beth remembered, with a shock, that at least one person was sorry for Mr Lamb's death – Mrs King's sister, Cheryl's Auntie Gina.

They found Cheryl lying on the sofa with a rug over her knees. The room was dim because the curtains were still closed, and the TV set was playing softly in a corner.

"Hello," she said in a little voice.

"How are you, Cheryl?" Jo asked kindly.

"Let's have a bit of light, for heaven's sake," said Beth briskly. She went to the green velour curtains and pulled them apart. "It's a beautiful day. You don't know what you're missing."

The sunlight, filtered by the net curtains, lit up the room with a soft diffused glow. Cheryl blinked. Her long fair hair was dishevelled and there were dark circles under her eyes.

"Oh," she protested, "don't! I had a dreadful night."

Beth was unrepentant. "I didn't sleep all that well myself," she said tersely. She was sick of the dull ache of worry that was part of her every waking moment since yesterday. She wanted action now. Cheryl must know something that she wasn't saying. It was her drawing in Mr Lamb's hand, after all. She sat down on the other end of the sofa. She wasn't Toby, she wasn't going to protect her and 'calm her down'. Jo perched herself on the arm of one of the chairs.

There was something worrying Cheryl too, and she got there first. She studied Beth's face intently.

"Beth, did you . . . have you . . . does anyone. . . ?" She couldn't get it out. Beth knew what it was.

"That drawing of the sheep, Cheryl," she broke in. "Your drawing, how did it get there?"

Jo gasped. She hadn't known about the drawing, thought Beth with some relief. At least that's something.

"Have you told anyone it's mine?" Real fear looked out of Cheryl's blue eyes.

"No, actually I haven't – yet. I needed time to think about it a bit. I need to know why Mr Lamb had it in his hand like that."

"Please don't tell, Beth." Cheryl was pleading now. "We didn't mean any harm, really we didn't."

"We?"

"You know – the boys and me – we were only having a bit of fun. You saw."

"What did you do with the drawing after I left? How did Mr Lamb get to see it?" Beth demanded. If he saw it, my God, she thought, and he lost his temper, did they have a fight? Her mind fell over itself.

Cheryl shook her head.

Jo leaned forward suddenly. "Cheryl, you've got to tell somebody sometime. You'll only get into more trouble if you don't."

"What did the police want to know, anyway?" Beth put on the pressure. She could see panic just behind Cheryl's eyes. Her lips started to quiver. There was a long pause when they both stared at her.

"I promised Toby," Cheryl spoke at last. "Ask Toby." She was almost inaudible.

"Toby," Beth breathed his name. They had done something dreadful, she knew it. She had known it the moment they wouldn't tell her the truth at Toby's house. She glanced at Jo and saw that her friend had gone white again. Why? What did Jo know that she didn't? The jar of blood hidden under the top hat in Jo's costume room came back to her with a jolt. What was all that about? She must try to talk to Jo about it. There was something too odd about her behaviour to let it go.

Cheryl was sobbing softly and at that moment her mother came in with cups of tea and biscuits.

When she saw her daughter's heaving shoulders she put down the tray and hurried over.

"I think Cheryl's had enough now. Sorry, girls – time you were going. She's upset."

"*Bella*'s going on, Cheryl," Jo said as they stood up, hoping to comfort her.

"Hmm." Mrs King's voice hardened. "Without our Cheryl."

"Oh, Mum . . ." Cheryl's distress was complete. She threw herself back on the sofa and wept aloud. Beth and Jo left Mrs King trying to comfort her as they saw themselves out.

"To Toby's?" Jo asked as they went down the front path.

"To the café," Beth said. "We've got to think this through."

A man stepped out and stopped them as they

were about to get on their bikes. He stood in front of them, barring their way.

"Are you young ladies members of the theatre group?" he asked them with a pleasant smile. He was about thirty-five, Beth guessed, clean-shaven, wearing slacks and a white shirt. His rather sporty anorak looked a bit out of place.

"We're SAPS," Beth answered him shortly. "Who're you?"

"Terrible tragedy, words can't express." He fished in his pocket. "*Tolford Guardian*." He showed them his press card.

"We're in a hurry," Jo said politely.

"I take it you're both friends of the young lady indoors," he indicated Cheryl's house. "I gather she collapsed during the police inquiry. Can either of you shed any light on this – why her in particular?" He raised his eyebrows suggestively.

"Well," Beth leaned forward confidentially and paused. The reporter whipped out a notebook from somewhere and put his pencil in his mouth as he flipped over to a clean page.

"She's allergic . . ." She paused again.

"Allergic to. . . ?"

"Nosey parkers!" Beth said very loudly and suddenly so that the reporter took a surprised step back and the girls were on their bikes and away before he could get his pencil back behind his ear.

"Spiked his guns!" Suddenly they were laughing, and it felt good.

7

MacHenry's – Mack's to all Tolfordians alike – had been the traditional meeting place for SAPS since time immi-mortal, as Sam called it. It was Tolford Regis's version of a hamburger joint. The owner, Mr Henry Coombes, called it MacHenry's in deference to, or in imitation of, the more famous chain of fast-food cafés. Along with hamburgers MacHenry's served other easy dishes and soft drinks as well as coffee and strong brown tea in thick china cups. That was where Henry Coombes diverged from his rival. No plastic in his café, no sir!

He had a longstanding relationship with the youth of Tolford. He treated them with an air of contemptuous disparagement and they returned this with quips of an equally disrespectful kind. Everyone knew where they stood. Should anyone be foolish enough to go over the line or cause a disturbance then Mr Coombes's large bulk and formidable weight were brought to bear. To be barred from MacHenry's was punishment enough.

It was just after three when Beth and Jo locked their bikes up and pushed open MacHenry's glass door. There wasn't a SAP in sight. Jo sat down at a window table while Beth went up to the counter.

"Two teas, please, Henry, and two buns," she said, their appetites sharpened by the long bike ride.

Henry put down his newspaper and looked at her.

"Dire doings at The Tree," he said, as he reached for the cups. "Any suspects?"

Beth shook her head.

"Not a popular man, that Lamb," Henry went on laconically as he poured the tea. "Funeral Thursday."

"Umm." News travels fast in this town, Beth thought.

"You're talkative today." Henry pushed the tea and two plates with buns towards her. "I hear you found him."

Beth fished out her money. "Yes," she said.

Henry took it. He clenched his fist and brushed her cheek with a clump of hairy knuckles. "Keep smiling, girl!" he said and got the grin he was working for.

"What's the matter with you?" he shouted to Jo. "Lost the use of your arms, or do you think your friend here has an extra?"

"I can manage. Shut up, Henry!" Beth balanced the plates of buns on the cups and crossed the room.

Henry Coombes put his head on one side and watched her. He had a lot of time for Beth. Can't have been a load of laughs, he thought.

The café's door flew open and Fiona McLaren came in with a rush, followed by another new SAP called Tracy Catchpole. Steve Marsh followed more slowly. He was a large, heavy boy, immensely strong.

"Hi, you two!" Fiona sang out, seeing Beth and Jo. "D'you want company?"

They didn't. They wanted to talk about their visit to Cheryl.

"Well, actually . . ." Jo began.

Too late. Fiona had organized Steve and he was getting their orders. The two girls plonked themselves down in the empty chairs at the table.

Blast! thought Beth. That Fiona – you wouldn't think she was new to this production.

Jo sipped her tea quietly. She watched the newcomers, her expression guarded.

"I heard . . ." Fiona leaned across the table and

lowered her voice dramatically. "Someone told me that . . ." she paused again.

"Get on with it," Beth rolled her eyes.

"Well, it transpires . . ." Fiona was from Scotland and she rolled her rrrs ferociously, "that Gary Smith quoted *Macbeth* in the theatre on Saturday, twice!"

"So?" Beth didn't give anything away. Who on earth told her that? she was thinking.

"Well," Fiona said again. "And look what happened! Murder!" She sat back as if to say, What else should one expect?

"For God's sake, Fiona," Beth saw Tracy Catchpole's eyes widen, "do you really think that's why Baa-Baa was killed?"

Steve brought the cups of coffee, put them down and stood awkwardly.

"Well, it's a very strange coincidence, isn't it? Oh, for goodness' sake, Steve, pull up a chair or something. You see," she dropped her voice again, "I happen to be psychic."

"That's all we need," Beth muttered.

"My family are all what we call 'fey' at home in Scotland. I knew, I just knew something dreadful was going to happen as soon as I entered the theatre on Saturday."

"Then why," Jo put in too sweetly, "didn't you say so at the time?"

"Well, I didn't know what it was, did I? I

couldn't go around alarming everyone, could I?"

There was no answer to that.

"I wouldn't be surprised," Fiona went on happily, oblivious of her unresponsive audience, "if Bella Gardoni's ghost doesn't make an appearance now. She's supposed to walk if there's something wrong at The Tree, isn't she?"

"She doesn't 'put in an appearance', as you put it," Beth said coldly. "If you knew the legend," she went on pointedly, "but you're new and you probably don't, Bella's ghost is never seen. She just leaves a trail of perfume behind her – her favourite flower . . ." Beth tried to remember which flower.

"Stephanotis," Jo supplied. "Mine too."

"Ah . . . yes . . ." Beth breathed and her hand rose unbidden to her mouth. "What does stephanotis smell like, Jo?" she asked urgently. Was it anything like cleaning fluid?

Fiona's eyes gleamed. Beth's expression hadn't gone unnoticed.

The café door swung open again. Rob entered and held it open for Antonia. They didn't look towards the others but made for a centre table. Fiona swivelled round when she saw them. Beth nudged Jo under the table. "Now what?" she muttered.

Without a pause Fiona rose. "There's Rob," she said unnecessarily. "There's a bit in my part I want to discuss with him." Fiona was playing Bella's younger sister – she could look about twelve if she tried. Right now she was trying to look seventeen. She was actually fifteen-and-a-half.

"Come on, Tracy," she swept towards the centre table with Tracy in her wake. Steve was left behind looking awkward and uncertain what to do.

"Don't mind us, Steve," Jo said kindly. She liked the big, amiable, rather slow boy. "Carry on over if you want to."

Beth smiled at him encouragingly. With relief he rose and gathered up the three coffees. He muttered, "See you!" and went to join the group in the centre.

"So much for Rob's quiet moment alone with his leading lady," Beth muttered to Jo under her breath. "I wonder if the boys will turn up next?"

Jo leaned forward abruptly. "Beth, what's this about Cheryl and that drawing? What do you know?"

"The boys and Cheryl were planning something. But you knew about that, didn't you? The drawing was part of it."

"No," Jo said flatly. "I didn't know."

Didn't know what? About the drawing or about the plot?

Beth hesitated. Should she tackle Jo on the subject of the jamjar of blood again? It didn't seem such a big deal. Jo had only denied having it when she had had it all the time. It could have been a moment's forgetfulness, after all. It really wasn't much. Jo wasn't a liar . . . was she?

Beth put it away from her and their two heads met over the table.

"Gary and Toby made the blood and I heard them talking about a blood sacrifice. Then Baa-Baa turns up dead with the blood all over him – and probably some of his own—" Beth shuddered. The moment returned, vividly. She was standing with her hand on the light switch in that pool of . . . was the dark shadow round his head only shadow or. . . ?

Jo put her hand on her arm. Beth went on with an effort. "And he had Cheryl's drawing in his hand. Now she's frightened out of her wits – you saw her too – and says Toby'd made her promise not to talk about it."

"Ah," said Jo softly.

Beth was following her own thoughts. What had happened to that bucket of blood? That's what she wanted to know. When she left The Tree it had all been tidied up. There was no sign of it. She remembered thinking that was a change – it was usually up to her to sweep up at the end of each session. How on earth had it ended up all over dead Baa-Baa? It was no good. She just had to ask.

"Jo," she said suddenly, "*when* did you get some blood for your costumes?"

With a sinking heart Beth watched her friend's face go stiff.

MacHenry's was filling up. Several more SAPS and a smattering of afternoon shoppers had filled nearly all the tables. The noise level rose and the girls were having to speak louder. The group at the next table turned to stare. Beth's question must have startled them.

Jo said calmly, "I think we'd better move. Listen, Beth, I've been thinking. Do you still have the keys to The Tree, or did you give them back to Paula?"

Beth, surprised by Jo's change of subject, found it hard to think. There had been such chaos at The Tree. They'd left Paula at the theatre after the police interviews. Everyone was in a hurry to get away in the end.

"If I have them, they'll still be in my basket. The police must be using Mr Lamb's set." She reached for her basket under the table. It went with her everywhere.

"If we're not meeting again till after Baa-Baa's funeral on Thursday, I'll just have to get some work to take home to be going on with," Jo went on. "It's Monday today. There'll be so little time after Thursday before the dress rehearsal. Could we go there, d'you think? It'd be quieter. Would anybody mind?"

"We'll go." Beth stood up. It would be quieter, that was true, and maybe she could think more clearly there. Was Jo trying to evade this blood issue? Or was she really worried about her beloved costumes? What seemed clear was that Jo was not going to admit that anything odd had been going on when she got the blood. But she must have got it at exactly the time when *everything* was going on. Hope came. Perhaps someone had brought the blood to her. That way she wasn't lying. It was so important to Beth that Jo was not lying.

The girls wheeled their bikes down Tolford High Street to the little square at the end where The Tree took pride of place. They followed their usual path round to the back and stopped. A policeman stood outside the scene dock door.

"Come on," Beth said with relief. "It'll be all right. I met him on Saturday. He's been a SAP, would you believe!"

The tall young policeman with ginger hair and freckles looked down on them. "Hello," he said. "Come back to the scene of the crime?"

"That's not very funny," Beth told him.

"No, it wasn't, you're right." He looked very contrite. "I'm really sorry. Beth, isn't it?" he said.

"What do we call you?" Beth asked him, forgiving him on the spot. She remembered his attempts to be kind to her.

"I'm PC Daniels," he said. "But you can call me Mark."

Beth introduced Jo. "Our famous costume SAP."

Mark Daniels looked at her and smiled.

Most men smile at Jo like that, Beth reflected wryly. What a good thing I'm not a jealous type.

It was true. Beth knew Jo was beautiful. She wasn't flashy, but had a grace and quiet loveliness that spoke volumes. Beth loved her for it and for the gentle nature that went with it. That wasn't to say that Beth had never felt the pangs of envy as they grew up together. Of course she had. But her affection and steady humour usually sent them packing.

It was a fact that Jo never noticed the effect she was having when men smiled at her. She just smiled back and always looked straight into their eyes when she did this. This time her amber-coloured eyes were looking into blue-grey. Beth noticed they were nearly the same height.

Suddenly, without any warning at all, she was gripped by a strong twinge of jealousy to be followed quickly by a jumble of other emotions – confusion mainly. What was it about this particular smile from this particular face that had brought that on? She hated feeling like that, especially with Jo. She hadn't quite sorted out the last time – only yesterday – with Toby and Cheryl. Was she falling apart?

An appalling suggestion came unbidden. What if Jo had smiled at Baa-Baa like that? Did he mean Jo when he spoke of her 'sexy friend'? She had thought of Cheryl right away, but . . . The thought made her feel sick. I need to wash my mind out with soap and water, she scolded herself. But once you've thought something, Beth realized, it sticks, and there was the mystery of the jar of blood.

And what's more, her inner voice continued, I still have no idea what they were all up to!

Beth made a resolve. If she was being asked to keep the secret about that drawing she was going to know exactly what had gone on and what the plotters had done after she had left the theatre. She would tackle them all tomorrow.

"I need to pick some costumes up," Jo was saying. "There's such a short time to the show."

"We won't touch anything. You can come in with us," Beth said quickly.

PC Daniels hesitated.

"Once a SAP, remember?"

Mark gave in. "SAPS against the world!" he said and opened the door for them.

8

They walked through the familiar theatre rooms quietly. PC Daniels took them to Jo's costume room and then left them to sort out what she needed.

Beth shut the door of the tiny room. She needed to be secret. It felt stuffy and smelt of dust but she just had to have it out with Jo.

"Jo, out with it — come clean about that blood," she said.

"Clean?" Jo's face had that look again.

"When did you go and get it?"

"Actually, Sam came and told me it was ready." Jo gave a little shrug as if to imply that Beth was fussing.

"Sam?" Why Sam?

"Yes, he seemed very excited about something and was quite insistent that I had to get the stuff right away. He was so proud of it I thought he'd made it."

"Toby and Gary made it," Beth chipped in.

"I found that out later, but you know how Sam likes to impress. Anyway, I got a jamjar from the cupboard and went with him."

"Was the bucket still on the floor of the scene dock?"

"Yes, near the prop gallery."

"And who else was there?"

"Heavens, Beth! Talk about the third degree . . ."

"Were the other two and Cheryl still there?" Beth pressed on.

"They left just as I came in. Cheryl was waving a piece of paper and I remember thinking she was rather hyped up. I suppose," Jo said slowly, "she was going off to do that drawing. I didn't know that at the time."

"Why were you so vague and funny when I asked you about the blood?" Beth demanded.

Jo hesitated. "Well . . . I was thinking about Sam and not listening properly. He's such a . . . there's something so touching about him."

"Pathetic, you mean." Beth couldn't guess how Sam had got into this.

Jo frowned. "No, Beth, I don't mean pathetic." She spoke quite sternly. Beth blinked.

"I really like him. Under all that jumping about and boasting there's a really sweet person."

This was certainly not what Beth had expected to hear and she blinked again.

"Jo Henly, only you would say a thing like that. You gather lame ducks to you like some mother hen." Beth was exasperated. "Sam's OK, he's part of the group and good for a laugh, but he can be such a pain."

Jo turned away and began to stuff garments into a plastic bag. Beth couldn't tell now what she was feeling.

Bother Sam Forrest! she thought. Why has Jo come over all protective?

Sam was small and wiry, with dark hair and a sallow complexion. He had the sort of skin that erupted in acne constantly. As an actor he brought life and character to his roles. As a friend he was erratic and inclined to shoot off the handle but when on top form he was magic. He lived in a run-down block of flats near the railway with his older brother. Their mother had left them when the boys were small, and now his father was doing time for some petty crimes he kept repeating.

Sam was very conscious of his background. In his attempt to keep his place in the group he often pushed too hard.

Beth thought about it. Could a complicated character like that go for murder? She remembered the scene when Baa-Baa had caught him keyholing outside the boiler room. She would never forget Sam's defeated face after Lamb had let him fall with such contempt. Lamb bullied him unmercifully. How much could a guy like Sam take? Come to think of it, Jo had been first on that scene, she remembered.

"Baa-Baa was wicked to him, you know," Jo spoke again, still turned away and busy. It was almost as if she had read Beth's thoughts. "Didn't you notice? He put him down on every front. He never let him forget about his dad – or let us forget. He never let Sam forget how small he is, either. Sam couldn't take that. There are many ways in which Sam isn't small at all."

Another memory rushed into Beth's mind: Mr Lamb, large, strong and very macho, holding a furious Sam at bay with one long arm pushed against his chest. Sam's fists were flailing helplessly centimetres from Lamb's face. She remembered his laughter and Sam's gasping breaths. Lamb must have been goading him on. Of all the group Sam needed to be on top and Baa-Baa always cut him down to size. Perhaps Sam had just had enough . . .

"Sam told me, while I was scooping up the blood," Jo's quiet voice went on, "that he had had an idea that would shut Baa-Baa up for good." Beth's eyes widened with horror, but Jo didn't seem to realize what she had said.

"I just thought that he was trying to impress me. You see . . ." Beth watched Jo's controlled movements as she continued methodically gathering up her spools of thread, scissors and box of pins and placed them carefully in the bag on top of the costumes. Jo at her most calm often meant Jo most inwardly disturbed. She couldn't imagine what was coming.

"Sam came in here, that time when we were doing *Maria Martin*. I had just stuck a needle into Lamb's arm."

"You'd what?" Beth thought she hadn't heard right.

Jo went on quietly. "He was jumping around all over the place – and swearing." The smallest twitch of a smile played round her mouth.

"Why, for goodness' sake?"

"He tried to . . . kiss me." Still the same calm voice went on. "He got me by my hair and . . . I stuck my needle into his arm!" This last was said with a low intensity that made Beth gasp. Jo's face had gone quite still, like an alabaster carving. Beth had never seen her look like that. It was a deep, cold hatred of a look. Beth shivered. In her mind's eye she saw an outraged Lamb grabbing at his forearm, bellowing and howling with anger and pain while Jo watched, cold and motionless, with that shadow of a smile on her lips.

"It hadn't been the first time," Jo's calm voice

continued. "I didn't always have a needle on me."

"Jo!" Beth breathed, horrified at what she was hearing. "You never told me."

"No." Jo let out a deep breath. "Only Sam knew. Baa-Baa never allowed him to forget that either, and Sam never said anything to anyone. That was difficult for Sam. He's not the best with secrets. He knew I would have killed myself if anyone else had found out."

Beth gasped. Jo was implying more than kissing.

"I mean it, Beth. You've got to believe me. If you tell a soul, I'll . . ."

"I won't. I won't. I promise, Jo." Somehow Beth had to bring her back from that cold, icy place she was in. Cold, icy and remote. Untouchable. Unrecognizable.

"Sam did well," she said helplessly.

To her great relief she saw Jo's face soften.

"Yes, he did." Jo turned her face to her friend. Beth saw with some relief that her eyes were their usual clear honey colour but very troubled.

"But Jo," Beth spoke gently, "let's get back to Saturday."

Jo sighed deeply. "On Saturday Sam told me how much he . . . liked me, admired me, and wanted to go out with me, and . . . I don't know what to do." Jo sat down suddenly and put her face in her hands.

"You mean, you don't want to hurt him, or. . . ?"

Light was beginning to dawn. Or was it that she was afraid that if she didn't go out with him he would forget to keep her secret? Either way was fraught with problems.

"All that." Jo waved a limp hand. "But also, I never know how far Sam will go to make himself feel big, especially if he wants to impress someone special to him."

"You mean you, don't you?"

Jo nodded. She looked miserable.

Oh, you idiot! Beth said to herself. How can you be so slow? She's telling you she's afraid that Sam Forrest might have killed Lamb for all those reasons, and one of the reasons is her.

"Never fear, nemesis is near," she found herself repeating. She leaned across in the small space and put her arm round Jo. "I'm going to get to the bottom of all this, see if I don't," she said. Brave words, Beth, she mocked herself.

"And anyway," she added softly, "it wasn't Sam's idea, it was Toby's." She felt like a traitor.

"Ah!" Jo began to fill another plastic bag. "You can carry this one on your bike for me, can't you?" Suddenly she was all practical and businesslike.

"Sure." Beth opened the door, glad to be thinking ordinary thoughts again. "There's something I want to do, Jo. I'll see you outside, OK?"

"OK."

Beth passed through the door into the green

room and paused away from Jo's familiar presence. She did have something she needed to do but Jo's words had shocked her deeply. She had never seen her friend like that before, so – so deadly, there was no other word for it. She knew Jo's loyalty and kindness was genuine, she had experience of it herself and loved her for it. But what exactly had Lamb done to her that she would kill herself if it came out? Beth realized that was not an idle threat. Jo meant it. Quiet, calm, purposeful Jo could have been brought to the brink. Was she now trying to implicate Sam? Or trying to protect him?

Oh, God, I'll think about that later, she decided in desperation, standing in the middle of the green room searching for reassurance from the familiar place and taking in its shabby chairs, sink and electric kettle, conglomeration of mugs, cluttered noticeboard and balding carpet. The scene on Sunday morning had been anything but familiar. Then the friendly room was full of fear and confusion. Would nowhere ever seem the same to her again? It had been full of people trying to make sense of what had been found on their stage, in their space. That fear and confusion had not gone away, and it wouldn't until they had discovered who had killed Mr Lamb. Who had deliberately put a stage weight in a bucket of stage blood and dropped it on his head? Beth expected the police were digging away at the mystery. But she was aware that she knew certain facts they did not. This would give her a head start if she cared to take it, and she had to. Too many of her close friends were touched by it. She had to get to the answer before too much damage was done.

The blood was in the centre of it – no, she quickly corrected herself, unpleasant, unspeakable Baa-Baa was in the middle of it all. The blood stood for the hatred he had inspired.

The bucket had to be taken up the steps onto the lighting gantry that ran down both sides of the stage and across the back. This assisted the stage staff to use the theatre flies by hoisting furniture and scenery up there with the aid of ropes which were then tied off. A counter-weight system was also in use for the heavier things. The flies were deep enough so that anything lifted that way could be tied off out of sight of the people in the front row of the stalls. Also, the lighting bars that crossed the stage suspending their banks of lights could be adjusted from there and spotlights or large floods fixed in place along the length of it.

Someone had to walk from the scene dock, carrying the bucket in the first place. Beth tried to reason it out. They walked through the green room and up the stairs to the stage. There was no other way. Then they had to climb the narrow gantry steps. It was quite a journey. I wonder if anybody saw them doing any part of it?

If the costume-room door was open, Beth's reluctant mind dragged on, Jo could have seen. And if Jo knew the plot and wanted to take advantage of it she was ideally placed to do so. But Jo was shielding Sam, and Sam was keeping Jo's secret and hated Lamb, so where did all that lead her? Round in circles.

And then there's that drawing . . . She was talking to herself again. I've got to go up there.

Stopping herself thinking any more, Beth turned through the green-room door and belted up the stairs to the stage. She arrived in her prompt corner breathing quickly.

And then, she told herself, I looked for the light switch, here, on the pillar, and turned it on. Click. The strong white light washed the area. The wing curtains, or legs, cast long shadow bars across the open stage.

Beth forced her eyes to look down. A dark stain spread around her feet and the horror returned in force. She was rooted to the spot, her shoes bedded in concrete.

"It's only water, Beth," a voice came from behind her and she nearly died. She spun round.

"The stage has been scrubbed. It's only water," Mark Daniels spoke reassuringly. "I don't think you should be here, you know. Why are you?"

Beth couldn't tell him but the urge to do so was very strong. It was SAPS business. He had been a

SAP, it was true, but now he wore a uniform. He had other loyalties. Hers were quite straightforward. Her closest friends were all lumped together in this business, and she didn't know the half of it but she was going to protect them if it was the last thing she did! A bit melodramatic, her good sense told her, but this *was* melodrama, wasn't it? She must use this chance to look at the 'scene of the crime' with a clear head.

"Oh, I . . . just had to, somehow. To lay the ghosts . . . you know." She hoped Bella Gardoni wasn't listening. At least she wasn't smelling anything peculiar.

Just to the right of the light switch on the brick pillar Beth saw four torn shreds of masking tape. There was one at each corner of a square. They still had the corners of the paper they were pinning to the wall attached to them. In two places there was a sizeable fragment. Whatever had been there had been ripped violently off. She hadn't noticed it the first time but that must be where the drawing had been stuck before Mr Lamb had grabbed it. He would have grabbed at it – it was hideous.

PC Daniels' eyes followed hers and rested on the torn corners.

"Come away, Beth. Let the heavy mob sort all this out. They will, you know." He looked at her carefully. "I don't suppose," he said quietly, "you know a bit more about all this than you're letting on?"

She suddenly remembered the way his freckles had stood out against his white skin when he returned from standing right here looking at dead Mr Lamb. His was a hard job. She didn't suppose he'd been in it very long and she really wanted to be honest with him.

"Wish I did," she said. Almost true.

They turned away together.

As they passed the boiler room, Beth knew she had to go inside and have a look at it. If she was to sort this thing out she had to see everything. But first things first. Somehow her friends were going to tell her what she needed to know. How else could she help them?

Jo was sitting on the steps outside the stage-door entrance when they emerged. She looked like some exotic bag lady surrounded by her plastic bags of costumes. She also looked very tired.

Beth's heart filled with her old affection as she took in the familiar figure and she pushed her impatience to one side. "Help me strap one of those bags to my bike, please, Mark. No more excitement for us today," she said to Jo. "Come on, we're going home."

9

The following morning Beth headed for the telephone. She punched Jo's number. Jo was up to her eyes in sewing and wondered if Beth would like to help.

"Love to," Beth replied. "But you know I can't even thread a needle." This was not strictly true. Beth liked to foster a hopelessly inept image of herself when threatened with sewing. She hated it. She would spend hours restoring an old picture frame or a broken fan for a show, but the only sewing she would attempt was turning up one of the theatre curtains or something else where she could use huge stitches and get it done quickly. She was only just checking on Jo really, for she had other plans.

Next she phoned Gary. His younger sister answered and told Beth he'd already set off for Toby's house.

So Beth rang Toby. She was determined to speak to one of the boys. Although she intended to see them both if possible, she felt she really needed to get Toby alone if she could. She hadn't felt right about him ever since the unsatisfying gathering at his house after the police interviews. It was so unlike Toby to be that evasive – at least, with her. Put side by side with the way he and Cheryl had been behaving, it left Beth feeling a bit like a stranger.

She had to admit that Toby enjoyed Cheryl's flirting with him. It seemed so obvious to Beth that Cheryl was just setting her cap at one of the main actors in SAPS. Why couldn't Toby see this? Beth realized that she was clinging to the hope that it was just a game Toby was playing, and that he needed to shield Cheryl over this Lamb business to save all their skins. That when it was over things between them would settle down again. In the meantime she'd just have to guard herself from the sharp pangs of hurt that dug at her when she thought of them both.

"Beth? Hi!" Toby picked up the phone sounding, Beth thought, slightly wary.

"Toby," she said as casually as she could, picturing his familiar face below its shock of hair, "mind if I come over? I've got something to discuss – about *Bella*."

"Oh? What?"

"I'd rather see you. It's a bit complicated." She bit her lip. She hated lying.

"Actually, sorry, but I'm about to go out to do something for Dad. He's got some red tape to sort out over Baa-Baa's funeral on Thursday. As councillor in charge of The Tree and all that he has to oversee it. I said I'd do an errand for him. Will it keep?" He sounded concerned.

"Have to," said Beth. "I'll try again! 'Bye!" She spoke lightly but her heart had begun to feel like a lump of dough. The lying toad! she thought. How could he do that to her? That bit about the funeral . . . Anger rose in her. She grabbed her basket and made for the back door. In two minutes she was cycling furiously into Tolford.

Toby's head appeared around his front door in answer to Beth's ring.

"Oh," he said. "Beth."

"Hi, Toby! Can I come in?" Beth went into the hall, passing Toby's nonplussed expression.

Gary came to the kitchen door. "Hi, Beth!" he said, surprised. "I didn't know you were coming." He looked at Toby.

"Neither did Toby," Beth said a little grimly. There was a pause while she stood her ground and the boys tried to regroup.

"Er . . . do come in." Toby tried sarcasm.

Beth grinned and waited.

"OK. Have a cup of coffee. You look as if you're here to stay." He led the way to the kitchen. Two mugs of coffee were already on the table.

"Don't let me stop you going out." Beth could use sarcasm too.

Toby ignored it. "Take a seat and tell us what you're doing here." He wasn't very friendly and Beth's spirits took a lurch – downwards.

"Jo and I went to see Cheryl yesterday," she began.

Toby raised his eyebrows. "So?"

"She's had another visit from the police."

"So've we," said Gary. "You too?"

"I was out yesterday," said Beth, feeling she was getting nowhere.

"They were just trying to find out if we had anything more to add to our statements."

"And have you?" Beth said pointedly.

Toby and Gary said nothing.

Beth suddenly thumped the table with her fist, and the mugs jumped. So did the boys. "You *know* you have. You *must* have. You know that I know Cheryl did that drawing. You also know how it ended up in Baa-Baa's hand, but I don't. I'll start to tell someone what I know, and they'll soon know a lot more about you unless you stop being so . . . so . . . idiotic!" She ended rather lamely.

There was no response. She tried again, quietly.

"Look, this is what I know. You made the blood and you hatched a plot to do something with it to get at Baa-Baa. Cheryl did her drawing for reasons unknown but also to make it hot for Baa-Baa. When Jo took some blood for her cossies it was still in the scene dock. Sam Forrest was there as well. When I went home early I couldn't see it so I guess it had been moved for some purpose. Somebody put the stage weight into the bucket at some time and someone threw the lot on Baa-Baa's head. It had to have been done last thing before he closed the theatre as no one knew about it. Wait a minute . . ."

Beth remembered the position of Mr Lamb's body, and also the position of the remains of Cheryl's drawing next to the light switch. "Wait just a minute," she repeated. "He was probably turning off the light – but what was the drawing doing on the wall?"

Gary's glasses glittered as he leaned forward. "It was a lure," he said.

"Gary!" Toby spoke sharply.

"We knew he'd stop and look at it." Beth caught the look Gary turned on Toby. It was hard and bitter. Perhaps he cares more about Cheryl than he lets on, was the thought that flashed through her mind. He's very possessive about his beloved lighting box, so why not Cheryl too? But he's playing it as if he doesn't care. All the tension seemed to be making her inner radar work overtime.

Gary went on, his face relaxing. "It's pointless to keep this up. Beth's one of us, she hasn't told the police about the drawing, and anyway – she found the pig." His voice thickened as he spoke.

"Beth, we had to—"

"If we're going to tell her," Toby interrupted, obviously not pleased with Gary, "we'll have to get Sam. He has a right to be in on this and agree to it, and Cheryl too."

"Cheryl told me to ask you," Beth told him quickly. She didn't want Cheryl in on this – she'd be in danger of having hysterics all the time. "It's OK with her. Actually," she added, wanting to see the boys' reaction, "her mother's forbidden her to be in *Bella* now."

If she had hoped to surprise them into an unguarded or revealing remark she was unsuccessful. Their faces remained blank.

Toby moved to the phone to try to talk to Sam.

"Poor old *Bella*," said Gary with a shrug.

Beth said, "I know Sam hated Mr Lamb's guts, and with reason. So did Cheryl. I don't know anyone who liked the man, except Cheryl's aunt. I . . ." she was back in the passage with his beery smell, "I loathed him myself."

"He was a rotten bully," Gary said, his voice level. "He loved to get hold of people weaker than himself and squeeze them till they hollered. He liked that."

"Did he squeeze you?" Beth asked outright.

"He did everything he could to make my lighting difficult," Gary began calmly. Suddenly his voice flared and he hit the table with the flat of his hand. "He was impossible. Utterly petty. Sometimes he pretended to lose the key of the lighting box when I knew he knew where it was. You know the sort of thing, Beth – I complained to you often enough. Or he'd go in there and remove all the gels I'd just set so they'd have to be done again."

"For goodness' sake, why would he do all that?" It made no sense to Beth.

"Because he knew I couldn't report him and he loved having power over people."

"You couldn't?"

"No," Gary said, and his face darkened. Once more he saw Baa-Baa put his great shoulder to the lighting-box door and force it open. That day he and Cheryl . . . he remembered Cheryl's terrified eyes and Baa-Baa's pure, gloating delight.

"Naughty, naughty," he had chanted. "Little boy, little girl, birds and bees . . . Well, well, well!"

"Cheryl and I were messing about in the lighting box one time," he said to Beth. "And Baa-Baa came in."

"Messing about?"

"Yes, just having a bit of fun, you know."

They'd only been kissing a little, just playing really. They'd been talking about their hopes for their future. Both took theatre very seriously. Cheryl, dramatic to the last, was so afraid that her parents wouldn't allow her to go to Drama School – she even talked of running away if they didn't. Gary had heard of a stage management course that included lighting, and he wondered if it was worth staying on for A levels.

"Don't be so thick, Beth. Cheryl and I had been seeing a lot of each other that holiday." Gary paused, remembering the way she would tease him rotten and then fling her arms around him. Beth saw his mouth set in a straight line.

"We always had lots to talk about," he continued. "Life's never dull with Cheryl around."

"Probably not." Beth couldn't help the acid in her tone.

Gary didn't notice. He was reliving the moment when Cheryl, impulsive as ever, had leaned forward and taken off his glasses. She'd told him his eyes reminded her of the leader of some group she liked and traced his eyebrow with her finger, and he'd kissed her. It was great. Jealousy gripped him in a vice. Now she was making a play for Toby, who didn't seem to be objecting. She still enjoyed his admiration, true, but she didn't want his company any more. His hand, lying on the table, clenched into a fist.

"Trouble was," Gary went on painfully, "we'd locked the door." He couldn't remember now why he had, except perhaps to keep the world out of his special place, his lighting box. It wasn't his, of course – Baa-Baa wouldn't let it be. He kicked the leg of the table viciously.

"Baa-Baa had to break in – had to show off his brute strength."

Beth pictured it. Baa-Baa could dirty anything.

"Of course," Gary went on bitterly, anger and misery in his voice, "he threatened to tell Cheryl's parents about us and you know what they'd do. Cheryl would have to leave SAPS."

"Cheryl'll probably have to leave as it is now," Beth said unhelpfully.

Then she registered with a sinking heart the fact that here was yet another reason for Cheryl to fear and hate Baa-Baa, and for Gary too – he could never betray Cheryl. Baa-Baa had put the finger on all of them.

Toby came back as Beth was working this through.

"Sam's on his way. He seems to think it's OK if you know."

And you, Toby, she thought, noticing his drawn face with a twisting heart. Did Baa-Baa have something on you too? Or are you playing some game I don't know about? I've never known you so remote and secretive.

Aloud she said, "So, the drawing was to lure Baa-Baa to the light switch? He would have turned it off anyway."

"It was to make him stay there long enough."

"Otherwise," Gary said, "he'd just have switched off the light and gone too quickly."

"Too quickly for what?" Beth still hadn't got the picture.

Toby took it back to the beginning. "The plan was that we sacrificed the bucket of blood by pouring it over Mr Lamb as he stood underneath the gantry by the light switch. Cheryl's cartoon was to make Baa-Baa stop long enough to look at it for us to get our position, our aim, right. Get it?"

"We knew," Gary put in, "that he switched the light off last thing before going home. We hoped there'd be enough paint in the bucket to blind him so we could rush out of the theatre before he could see properly. It was a risk."

"What about the weight?" asked Beth. "The weight that actually killed him. Whose idea was that?"

Gary and Toby looked at her for a long, serious minute. She held her breath. Then Toby said quietly, "That's just it. It wasn't us."

"The plan was to mark the beast," said Gary, "not slaughter him. We hoped he'd have such trouble getting all the paint off that there'd be bits sticking to him for ages."

"Revenge would be very sweet," Toby rubbed his face with his hands. "He was a disgusting man. You only had to look inside his boiler room."

"You've been in there?" Gary was surprised.

"Once," Toby said shortly. Beth got the feeling he hadn't meant to say that.

"We weren't allowed in. Why didn't you say?"

"Forgot, I suppose. It was ages ago."

"What was it like?" Gary pressed him.

"If you must know, it was covered with filthy pictures. Just leave it, Gary."

Beth began to understand the implications of what they said.

"Perhaps," she spoke across them sharply, "it would be better if you told Detective Chief Inspector Armitage. This is too serious."

"We can't, Beth," Toby's restless fingers pulled themselves through his hair. "Don't you see? One, they're bound to think that one of us has done it. Or all four of us together. Two, we don't know who did it. Each of us says we didn't do it, but . . ." he took a breath, "one of us has to be lying. If we lie low and say nothing at all they aren't going to find out about any of it. After all, if our finger-prints are on the bucket that's only to be expected, isn't it?"

"We can't tell anyone, don't you see, Beth?" Gary spoke in an intense whisper. "The police are nosing about us as it is."

"Who threw the bucket?" Beth tried to sound calm.

"We didn't mean to throw the bucket, just the paint."

"Then what happened exactly?"

"Sam said the bucket seemed heavier than he expected but he had to throw the paint so quickly he didn't have time to notice. It jerked itself out of his hand, bucket, paint and all."

"Sam?"

"We drew lots. Sam got the paper with the cross on it. He seemed thrilled to bits!" Gary snorted ironically.

So it was Sam who threw the paint. Beth remembered what Jo said: Sam wants to impress, needs to be the hero. After letting Jo take the paint out of the bucket did Sam replace the liquid level by sliding in the weight? Perhaps he was the one who carried the bucket up to the gantry, so no one else would have noticed how heavy it had become.

Beth's head began to spin. It was one thing thinking she was going to get to the bottom of the mystery, but now that she knew each of her friends might be suspected of murder, she felt desperate.

Toby's doorbell sounded loudly and they all jumped.

Sam, wearing a scarlet T-shirt and with his yellow baseball hat turned back to front, bounced into the kitchen and perched on the table.

"Hiya, Bethikins!" he said. "How's the sleuthing business?"

Toby sat down again and pushed his chair out, propping his feet on the table and crossing his arms as if to say, "Over to you, Sam." Gary took his glasses off and polished them on the tail of his black sweatshirt. Beth sensed a wary, guarded feeling between the boys – not just towards her, the inquisitor, but towards each other.

Toby's words, "One of us has to be lying," hung in the air between them.

"Sam," said Beth, trying to cut through his dreadful jauntiness, "why didn't you notice the bucket was heavier when you carried it to the gantry?"

Sam looked taken aback. "I didn't carry it. Toby did."

"I did," said Toby, "and it wasn't."

So, the weight was put in the bucket after it was taken to the gantry, if Toby spoke the truth. That was a move forward.

"I threw it," Sam declared, not wanting to have his thunder stolen.

"Then what?" Beth asked.

"Then nothing. We scarpered."

"Cheryl was with you all the time?"

"Sure. She wanted to see Baa-Baa's face when he found her drawing of him. He tore it off the wall. That was the last thing we saw."

"That was the last thing he did," said Beth, except for turning off the light, she thought. Then the sheet of red drenched him, and the heavy drop of the weight felled him. Death in the dark. She pushed the ever-constant picture of his splayed body away from her.

"You never saw him after that, but I did."

"So you did." Even Sam looked serious.

"When did you do all this?" she asked everyone at large, trying not to notice that none of the boys could meet her eye.

"After Jo got her blood and Cheryl did her drawing." Toby dragged his nail along the table, remembering the sequence. "I went to get Sam to see the drawing – he was still in the scene dock . . ."

"What were you doing, Sam?" Beth interrupted.

"I think I was just giving the paint a bit of a stir. Jo had left and I was longing for the fun to begin."

Toby continued. "After I told him that bit of the plan he went to look at the drawing in the star dressing room and I took the bucket straight up to the gantry to wait until we were all ready."

"Would you have noticed if the bucket was heavier than you expected?"

"I didn't put anything in it!" Sam protested.

Toby ignored him. "Oh, I think I would." But he didn't look too sure.

"Come on, Toby!" Sam jumped to his feet. "That's idiotic. A stage weight is heavier than a bucket not quite full of paint, for goodness' sake! What are you trying to do?"

"I'm not trying to do anything. I wasn't thinking about weight and paint at the time, that's all."

"You could have put the weight in yourself when you took it up. There are always stage weights lying about on the gantry."

Sam was going red in the face.

"Oh, sit down, Sam," said Gary, coldly. "And shut up!"

Sam threw himself into his chair, pushing it back so the legs scraped the tiled floor. He looked daggers at Toby.

Taking no notice of Sam's anger, Toby continued.

"It seemed the best time to do it. The place was empty, the rehearsal was in full swing, and we thought we could take a chance."

"*You* could take *your* chance, you mean," Sam muttered under his breath.

Toby went quite still.

"Leave it, Sam." Gary glared at him. "You and Toby weren't the only ones with the opportunity, you know."

Beth put that statement to one side. She didn't want to lose track of the sequence of events.

"I must have been in with Jo when you took the bucket up, Toby." She brought them back to the point. "So that you were down again by the time I found you all in the dressing room laughing over the drawing." As she spoke the thought that Jo could have slipped up the gantry steps at that point slid into her mind . . . But Jo had said she didn't know about the whole plot. Was that true, or did Sam tell her about it? Gary was right – the bucket had been up there long enough for everyone to fill it with weights!

She pulled herself together.

"OK," she continued. "Cheryl went to the wings with the drawing in her hand. She must have taped it up when she got the chance, and as I wasn't around that was easy."

"Clever old us!" Sam felt good again.

The others said nothing. Toby was reliving the moment when they had hidden themselves up on the gantry after the rehearsal was finished and everyone was going home. No one saw them creep up there. He could still feel the repressed excitement that vibrated through them as they tried not to giggle, tried not to attract attention.

Mr Lamb locked the outside door at the back of the stage. The theatre had three exit doors: the scene dock, the front doors and the stage door. This also opened on to the car park down a short flight of steps. Then he walked across the stage to the light switch near the prompt corner, just below where they were standing.

All his life, Toby thought, he would see the top of Baa-Baa's head, with its dark, thinning hair. Mr

Lamb was proud of his wavy hair and tried to cover the balding bits by brushing strands over them. Toby had relished the thought that those choice locks would soon be drenched red and sticky. They watched Baa-Baa pause, his hand out for the switch, and peer at Cheryl's drawing. They saw his other hand go out to it and take it by the top, ready to rip it off as rage gripped him. It had done what they wanted – it had stopped him long enough in one place.

Sam had moved like greased lightning. He'd seized the bucket and hoisted it up and over in one smooth movement the very moment the light went out. The fact that he'd dropped the bucket as well as the paint didn't matter.

They hadn't stopped to look. Like the four conspirators they were they'd scooted down the stairs to the empty green room and out of the scene dock as fast as they could, to giggle helplessly in the car park. They'd just squeezed into MacHenry's in time for a late Coke – a celebration. As far as anyone knew they had left Baa-Baa drenched in red paint with a bump on his head from the bucket as a bonus.

Beth looked at her friends and felt her energy drain away.

"Wow!" She let out a long breath. "Now what?" She couldn't go to the police, that was clear.

"We lie low," said Sam.

"But we can't let it go like that." Beth's reasoning powers were beginning to return. "Somebody murdered Baa-Baa. We all believe what each other says, but, who knows, we may be wrong to do so. All of us will suffer if the truth isn't discovered. And worst of all, you lot will never be free of it – ever. We'll never be the same again."

They thought about it. Beth was right, their position was intolerable. Already their friendships were being tested. Suspicion was a dreadful burden for them to have to carry.

"It's two weeks, less now, to the show. We can't go back to the theatre until the funeral's over, it'd look odd, so that makes it Friday." Beth was thinking out loud.

"When we do get back in . . ." She was going to say we must keep our wits about us, but she stopped abruptly. There wasn't a "we" any more, it was each for himself until they knew the truth, if they ever did. Any plans she made she must keep to herself – she couldn't even tell Jo.

"Well, when we do get back in," she said aloud, "we'll just have to get our skates on."

The boys nodded glumly. "Yeah."

Sam spoke up. "Anyone coming to Mac's? I'm starving." He got no response.

Beth got up. "I'm off home. See you on Friday."

"I want to get in early, Beth – lots to do." This was Gary. "Will you still have the keys?"

"Don't know," she answered. "I'll ring you." She wanted out now, fast. "'Bye," she said, and headed for the door.

Toby scrambled to his feet to let her out. She heard Sam's voice float after her. "Don't forget, Bethikins. SAPS against the world . . ."

Beth took a deep breath of warm summer air. Why did the world look so normal and safe when she knew it was anything but? Toby's front garden basked in a mid-morning glow. All along the side of his avenue the trees were fragrant and lush with leaves. Normally she would have biked home against the light breeze with her heart and hopes high, but now . . . what now? She might as well face it. One SAP, one of her friends, was probably a killer.

10

As Beth approached her gate a figure detached himself from the wall he had been sitting on.

"Miss Beth Greene?" he asked.

Beth recognized the *Tolford Guardian* reporter.

"Please, Miss Greene," the man said as Beth struggled to get her gate to open. "It's only my job, you know, and you do have a responsibility."

"Responsibility?"

"I didn't realize, when I met you yesterday, that you were the young lady who found the body. You have a responsibility to our readers. They'll want to know the truth."

Beth felt helpless. Truth!

"I told the police at the time," she said. "I've nothing more to say."

"How did you feel when you saw the dead man?" The question came quite simply, with no undue emphasis. He could have been asking how she felt about anything.

"Sick." What was the matter with the gate catch?

"You mean, you were sick?"

"No, I wasn't – oh, look, I don't want to talk about it. OK?"

"Have you any idea who might have done it? Did any of your friends bear Mr Lamb a grudge? He wasn't very popular, I hear."

"I don't know anything. I just found him. Now please go away."

This time Beth managed to get her gate to open and she pushed the bike through. The reporter called after her retreating figure, "Thank you, Miss Greene. You've been very helpful."

Beth didn't know if he was being sarcastic or not – had she said anything she shouldn't? She couldn't concentrate. She'd have to do better than that.

That evening two plain clothes policemen paid her a visit. They didn't stay long but went over old ground with her and seemed particularly interested in what she knew about Mr Lamb's activities away from The Tree. As she didn't really know very much about that part of his life there wasn't much she could tell them.

Some time during the night she woke suddenly out of a deep sleep and realized she'd been dreaming of Jo's orchard. She, Jo and all her close friends in SAPS were having a picnic. The sun was bright and they were happy in each other's company. Suddenly a black sticky substance began to fall from the branches of the tree above them. It smelled awful and polluted everything they were about to eat.

Paula Barton was there too and she said, out of the blue, "And we open tomorrow . . ." After which pronouncement Beth was so overcome with mingled disgust and anxiety that she woke up thankfully. She slept only lightly after that.

Wednesday inevitably followed Tuesday. True to form, after one day of sun, the summer weather dished out a day of squally rain. In the afternoon Beth pulled herself out of the lethargy that threatened to engulf her and got on her bike. She tied her hood on firmly and pedalled hard against the buffeting wind. By the time she had reached MacHenry's she was pink in the face and feeling a bit better.

Henry greeted her windswept self with a remark to the effect that she looked like something that had come in on a high tide, and she replied that if he got off his bum a bit more often he'd be able to get through the door – with luck. Honour satisfied on both sides, she picked up her Coke and looked around the room to see who was there.

It wasn't very full. There was a crowd of SAPS round the centre table (that was normal), two ladies and a pushchair by the window, and no one else.

"Bethikins!" Sam's head appeared over the others round the crowd on the centre table. "Over here!"

Beth hesitated. She could see Fiona and Tracy Catchpole there and Steve and two others with their backs to her. They looked intent on something that Fiona was doing. She was holding Steve's hand in front of her on the table. Steve was looking embarrassed. His face was bright red.

After yesterday Beth wasn't sure she wanted to be drawn into a group like that. She wasn't sure that she was all that pleased to see Sam, either. Jo might like him, but his everlasting chirpiness was getting on her nerves. He had as much reason as the others for hating the Lamb – was all this some sort of smokescreen? He was sitting next to Fiona, one arm on the back of her chair.

And he seems to be changing his devotion, she thought.

"Fiona's reading Steve's palm. She's ace!" Sam declared as Fiona positively purred with pleasure and importance. "She's done mine; why don't you get her to do yours?"

Fiona's voice rose just enough for Beth to hear. "You're a man of many parts, Steve," she said.

"That's true," Steve sounded impressed. He liked acting.

Beth raised her eyes to heaven. Fiona always seemed to have that effect on her. Maybe she could find the murderer in her own horoscope, she thought sourly.

"I'll sit over here," she said. "I've a book I want to finish. You lot will be crystal ball-gazing soon if Fiona has her way with you."

She sat down at a table and took her paperback out of her basket. The ladies with the pushchair were reading the local paper. Beth remembered that it came out on a Wednesday. She ought to get one, she supposed. The banner headline read TREE CARETAKER FELLED. In slightly smaller capitals she could see, SCHOOLGIRL BETH SAID 'I FELT SICK'. No, she thought, I won't get it. After all, I was there!

Fiona was talking about auras. Beth could hear her clear, pleasant voice telling the others what an aura was.

I bet she's been mugging all that up, Beth thought. She's a bit like Sam. She needs to feel the centre of everything. They should get together. On second thoughts, there'd be a collision if they did.

She opened her book, found her page and tried to read. She couldn't. Would Toby or Gary show up? She realized that this thought made her anxious – she actually didn't want to see any of them. Sam, Gary, Toby, Jo and Cheryl – they had all had the opportunity to get the weight into the bucket under the shadow and shelter of the dark gantry. It would only be the work of a moment. Toby alone didn't have a strong motive for doing anything more to Lamb than giving him a shock, at least as far as she knew. Her spirits began to ebb again.

Out of the corner of her eye she saw Paula Barton crossing the road. One hand held an umbrella and the other a bag of shopping. Even in the rain Paula still retained her glamour. She was wearing a red-belted mackintosh over black slacks. A black-and-white spotted scarf floated over her shoulder. Her head was bare and her dark brown hair smoothed back from her face and caught at the nape of her neck with something that glittered.

It wasn't that Beth wanted to be like Paula. One or two other SAPS wore their hair like her and tried to imitate her breezy, confident manner. Beth admired her and liked to be with her but never imagined she could look like her.

Paula was utterly different from other teachers she knew. She had come to teach drama at Tolford Regis's comprehensive school four years ago. As a youngster of twelve Beth had enjoyed her classes very much and had got drawn into SAPS two years later. When The Tree needed a new Creative Administrator Paula got the job. Robert Harris was on the board of governors of The Tree and their friendship started then. Beth knew Paula had been divorced and it had been rumoured that she had been ill before she came to Tolford, but that was all.

Anyway, Beth thought, it was a good day for Tolford Regis.

"I wondered if you'd be here." Someone had pushed MacHenry's door open and was standing in front of her.

"PC Daniels!"

"Shh! Incognito." He was wearing jeans and damp, blue anorak. His ginger hair was so short the rain had made it stand up in spikes instead of plastering it to his forehead. "I'm off duty."

He went to the counter and greeted Henry. It was obvious from his easy manner that he and Henry went back a long way. He lounged against the counter and played with an imaginary sheriff's badge on his front, demanding a Coke "in the name of the law". He used a phoney cowboy accent. It made Beth grin. He'd never make an actor.

Henry told him his big feet were stopping the view, so would he please sit down or he'd use him as a hatstand. Mark pulled an imaginary forelock and brought his drink over to Beth.

"May I?" he asked her, smiling and pulling out a chair.

Beth put her book away. Out of uniform he looked very young, and that smile of his was doing wonders for her ebbing spirits.

"Did you come here when you were at The Tree?" she asked.

"All the time. I was never an actor, you know, just a general dogsbody. I just loved being there."

"I know how it is." Beth smiled back. She could see the others craning their necks to get a look at who she was talking to and grinned to herself. I wonder how many here know he's a copper? she thought.

"How's the inquiry going?" She mustn't miss an opportunity.

"You're talking shop, you know," he raised an eyebrow.

"I know," she said, "but it's important."

"Well," he shrugged, "the big guns don't give a lot away. There's been masses of door-to-door questions and follow-up interviews. But they still don't know who did the drawing or exactly why it was stuck up there. They've narrowed it down to the lads who made the paint because that's their only connection really, but everyone's behaving like they don't know how to talk. The only thing they don't mind saying is that it happened to the right bloke."

Beth was silent.

Mark studied his finger ends. "It seems so odd."

"What does?" Beth asked him, thinking with relief that they weren't on the track yet.

"If someone wanted to murder anyone by dropping a stage weight on their heads, why would they bury it in a bucket of paint? It doesn't make much sense. Why not just drop the weight?"

"A good point, put like that."

"Unless . . . it was to cover their tracks and confuse the issue. Then it would make sense."

"Do you think the big guns have thought of that?"

"Bound to," Mark said, "if I have." Then he changed the subject firmly.

"How's your lovely friend with the costumes?"

Drat the girl! Beth thought, trying to laugh at herself as that sneaky stab of jealousy struck. There we go again. What was it about this damp, ginger-haired copper? She made herself think of Toby quickly and realized that it was a painful exercise where once it had been such a pleasure. There were too many question marks hanging over their relationship now. She knew he was hiding something important. You didn't have to be Brain of Britain to know that. Had she really known him at all? He could be devious, he could even be unkind, but surely never a murderer? Oh, Toby! She sighed inwardly, starting to ache.

Mark was watching her, waiting for an answer.

She pulled herself back to the present with an effort.

"My lovely friend with the costumes is at home working on them," she said, steering the conversation into general channels. Mark asked her all about the production and the company and Beth told him and asked Mark all about the police force and why he had joined and he told her.

"Beth!" She jumped. Their conversation had been engrossing.

Paula was leaning on a chair smiling at her. Beth hadn't seen her come in. Rain was dripping off her umbrella onto the floor. "I hoped I'd find you."

"Popular person," Mark Daniels grinned.

"Meet an old SAP. Paula Barton, Mark Daniels." Beth introduced them.

"Before your time, Mrs Barton, unfortunately." Mark stood up. "I must be off. 'The play's the thing' and all that. See you around, Beth. Good luck with *Bella*."

"'Bye!" Beth waved a hand as she watched his tall figue step out into the rain.

"Sorry to interrupt," Paula said. She stood her umbrella and shopping bag against the wall and sat down in Mark's empty chair.

"He looks a nice boy. What does he do?"

"PC Mark Daniels," Beth told her.

"Oh yes? Know him well?"

"No. He was the first on the scene after I phoned 999."

"Beth, you've had a bad time. Are you OK?"

"I guess so," she replied, glad of Paula's obvious sympathy.

"Was he on the hunt for clues?" Paula asked lightly.

"I'm not sure really." Beth wasn't. "He's nice anyway. What's up?"

"I forgot to take my keys back from you on Sunday. It's such a dreadful time. Robert – Mr Harris – is trying to set up an advertisement for a new caretaker but we won't get one until *Bella*'s over. Rob and I will alternate opening and shutting up until then. He'll be at The Tree for the day-to-day security. I'm doing Friday morning. You won't want to get there early again, not for a bit, will you?"

"Actually," Beth was glad of the chance to reply, "Gary and I were hoping to do that. Can we?"

"Well, if you're sure you won't get spooked."

"We'll be fine. I'm OK now. The dear old Tree's a good place and there's masses to do." A thought struck Beth. "Paula?"

Paula had been about to gather up her shoppng but she paused. "Yes?"

"When you took your aspirin in the green room on Saturday, you went out for a breather through the scene dock, right?"

"Sure."

"Was the bucket of blood still there?"

"I'm not sure I noticed," she replied. "I saw a group of SAPs but my head was thumping so. Why?"

"Did the police ask?"

"Well, I told them all I could. What's so special?"

"Oh," said Beth, shrugging a little. "It was gone when I went home so I just wondered."

"You don't know anything more about it all, Beth, do you?" Paula asked her seriously.

"Oh, no. I just can't help thinking round it, that's all."

"If you do," Paula persisted, looking her straight in the eyes, "you can tell me if you want to talk it over. I'm a SAP remember and, I hope, a friend."

Beth thought wistfully that there was nothing she would like better. Aloud she replied lightly, "If I solve the mystery you'll be the first to know, but truly, I'm as much in the dark as everyone else."

Fiona drifted past them on the way to the door. "Hi, Paula!" She stopped, paused dramatically with her hand on her breast and declaimed, "Act Two in the Legend of The Tree."

Everyone looked at her. She glowed.

"The ghost of Bella Gardoni meets the ghost of Mr George Lamb!" Fiona announced and swept out. Sam followed and paused at Beth's table.

"She's psychic, you know. Fiona's holding a seance tonight to contact Mr Lamb. She's going to ask him who killed him. Want to come?" He winked heavily at Beth. "Hi, Paula! 'Bye!" He went on his way after Fiona. The others followed, giggling.

"She's a menace!" Paula spoke involuntarily. Beth realized she was furious but then she gave a slight laugh. "I don't usually let Fiona get under my skin – still a bit jumpy, I expect."

"Personally, I'd like to . . ." Beth was going to say boil her in oil, but instead she laughed as well and said, "There's been enough violence done!" Then she added with an abrupt change of subject, "Are you going to go to his funeral?"

"Robert and I will be there, and any other SAP who wants to come."

"It's only down the end of my road," said Beth, "but I think I'll give it a miss."

Paula glanced at her quickly and looked away. "He wasn't . . . liked very much, was he?"

Beth tried to say it lightly. "Not a lot." Then she found herself asking Paula, "Did you like him?"

Paula looked away again.

What will she say? Beth wondered. After all, she is staff. I tend to forget.

"He was a . . . difficult man."

That covers a multitude, thought Beth.

"Well, then," Paula rose and reached for her umbrella. "See you Friday and – on with the show! Dear Beth," she added impulsively, "you're a rock. *Bella*'s lucky to have you."

Beth stared through the café window after Paula left, feeling warm and needed. It made a change! If *Bella* needed anyone, she mused, it was Paula Barton.

She was surprised to find that the shops were closing and rush hour beginning. Her mother would be on her way home by now. She was grateful to Mark for taking her mind successfully away from the things she didn't want to think about if only for a short while. After all, Mr Lamb's cremation was tomorrow and *Bella* would be on the road once more.

She went out. The rain had stopped and although there was still a stiff breeze blowing the air felt clean.

Beth's thoughts returned to Toby. Why did she get the feeling that something like the Great Wall of China was growing up between them? What must it be like, living with his father and unable to talk about it to him? Mr Harris was a puzzling man. Sometimes she had watched him being really possessive of Paula in front of Toby, as if he was aware that Toby saw much more of her than he did and he didn't like it.

Beth sighed. It was all such a muddle. She would love to talk to Toby by himself, like she used to, away from the others. They had been so easy together in the past. Now? She just wasn't sure of anything except that Toby didn't want to talk to her. Was it only because he was protecting Cheryl and the boys, or was there something more he had to hide?

11

The day Mr Lamb was cremated Beth went to Jo's house. The crematorium was just down the end of her road and she didn't want to be anywhere near it.

At Jo's, the girls listened to tapes and gossiped gently, talking about anything but their present crisis. For a short while Beth could make believe that nothing awful had happened in their world and that Jo's honesty hadn't been questioned. That morning everything was like it always had been.

Jo gave Beth simple tasks to do like glueing on hat braids and decorating bonnets with flowers. Little Beanie wandered in and managed to upset Jo's bead box, scattering the contents everywhere. Beth helped her find all the beads and put them back.

Towards the end of the afternoon, however, her mind began to stray, so she grabbed pen and paper and made herself lists of next week's jobs. When these were done she roved about in an aimless way until Jo found her absent-mindedly 'trimming' the long fringes on one of Bella's shawls. She took her sharp scissors out of Beth's hands.

"Go home," Jo told her, "and have a good night's sleep."

Beth gave in and got on her bike. At home she phoned Toby to find out what time he was called to rehearsal and if he was going to construct scenery after rehearsal next day. She really wanted to hear his voice. She did: she got his answerphone.

"Probably with Cheryl," she muttered bitterly.

To her surprise Beth slept well that night. Half past eight on Friday morning found her cycling hard towards The Tree. Gary was to be there at nine.

They didn't say anything to each other as they went into the darkened scene dock. Both were determined to keep any unwelcome thoughts about the murder well at bay.

Inside Gary said, "I need to get into the lighting box. Do you think Baa-Baa's keys are still in his room?"

"We'll look," she said.

They had never been allowed inside the boiler room and Toby's words had made them curious. In the summer the large old boiler was off most of the time except when hot water was wanted for a show. It was a reasonable sized room with a dusty, oily smell that made Beth want to sneeze. Like all the underground rooms it had a slit-shaped window high in the wall, otherwise it was lit by electric light. There was an office desk and chair with a noticeboard screwed on to the wall directly behind them. Next to the desk stood an old kitchen worktop and cupboard, where Mr Lamb had kept his tea- and coffee-making equipment. Dirty mugs lay around with stray cans of beer and other assorted oddments that a man might need for day-to-day occupation.

The walls were bare, but they hadn't been bare for long. They were covered with the remains of sellotape and blutack. It was obvious that once they had been covered with pictures of various sizes and shapes. "Filthy pictures," Toby had said.

Beth and Gary's joint imaginations lurched into action. Knowing Baa-Baa as they did they filled in the blanks with ease. The mere shadow of the man had left his mark on them.

"Wowee!" Gary breathed. "This must have been some picture gallery!"

"I wonder he was allowed." Beth was rooted to the spot, still feeling the presence of the man.

"No one came in here much. I don't expect Paula did."

"The police must have taken them. I wonder what they made of them?"

"Well," Gary pulled himself together, "they're probably used to it." He made for the desk. "Did he keep the keys here?"

Beth saw a line of hooks screwed into the noticeboard. They had individual keys dangling from them under labels. She read 'Lighting Box', and pulled a key off.

"Here," she held it out to Gary. "All the cupboard keys are here too for when the painters come. You go and do your thing and I'll sort out what I need."

"Right." Gary took the key but he didn't go. He turned it around in his hand thoughtfully.

"Funny to think Toby knew all about this and didn't tell us." He looked at Beth. "D'you think he knew something about Baa-Baa we didn't? He can be pretty close sometimes. Did you know he had a record?"

"Baa-Baa?"

"Toby. Our Toby was a juvenile delinquent!" Gary's smile looked more like a grimace.

Beth was stunned. Had he been that bad? But not now. Toby was different now.

Gary was watching her. Taking a step towards her, he said, "Beth, you know, I meant what I said the other day."

Beth couldn't remember. She was thinking of Toby.

"I really like you, you know. You're . . ." he searched for the right word, ". . . solid."

Anger rose in Beth. "Why, thanks a million, Gary!" she said with heavy sarcasm. "You're pretty opaque yourself!"

Gary didn't catch her tone. "No, I mean it, really, Beth." He took another step forward and Beth found herself backing into the boiler room's corner.

What's going on here? she wondered furiously. Does the shade of Mr Lamb still haunt his haunt?

Gary stretched out his hand and touched her cheek with his fingertips.

Beth came to life.

"Cut it, Gary!" she said sharply. Inside she was very angry with him. Gary might be fed up with Cheryl jilting him for Toby, but that was no reason for him to take it out on her.

Behind his glasses Gary's eyes went blank and he dropped his arm. He seemed uncertain what to do next.

Beth told him.

"Look," she began, trying to be calm, "it's tough, I know. First Cheryl, then Baa-Baa, but this just isn't on. Go and open your lighting box and keep your mind on *Bella*."

Gary gave a sigh and turned away. At the door he stopped. "If you feel . . . funny or anything, you know where I am.'' He said this in a rush and fled.

Well, of all the weirdos this side of the country! Gary was an intense, passionate person, Beth knew, and they liked each other, but there was something very odd about this. That sigh he gave as he turned away – was it disappointment, or could it have been relief? If she felt 'funny' at all it was because of what he had just told her about Toby. The Tree held no fears for her.

Beth looked around Baa-Baa's boiler room with distaste. Everything was grubby. A few notes were pinned to the board along with a year-planner showing the programme of events at the theatre. One of the drawing pins fixing it to the board had gone and a top corner was curling badly. Beth tugged at the desk drawers. Mr Lamb's personal things had obviously been removed, leaving an assortment of old plugs, screwdrivers, biros and buff envelopes lying jumbled in each one. The long central drawer was empty too except for a forlorn-looking paperclip.

Feeling dirtied by the sticky surfaces she had been touching, Beth reached over the desk for the rest of the keys she needed. The noticeboard shook a little as she did so and another drawing pin fell from the other top corner of the year-planner. Both corners being freed, it slumped forward and hung upside-down, pinned only at the bottom.

Beth stared. There was a square piece cut out of the noticeboard directly behind the planner. The hole it made went through to the wall. The shallow cavity was packed with something that had been carefully taped to the patch of wall.

It was obviously a hiding place, and a clever one at that. Certainly the policemen who had cleared the boiler room had never discovered it.

Beth leaned across the desk and reached out to undo the masking tape fixing the packet in place. She was intrigued. She lifted it down with care.

It turned out to be an exercise book that had been used as a scrapbook. Little strips of newspaper cuttings, some of them quite short, were stuck on the pages. Folded separately and lying inside the cover was the front page of an *Evening Standard* dating back five years. Its banner headline stood out large and black: BAG KILLER GETS LIFE. She read on:

Stanley Redman, the notorious Bag Killer, was sentenced to life imprisonment at the Old Bailey today. The man who stifled six people to death with plastic bags and kept the town of Holmsby in a state of terror for two years was at last brought to justice. An elderly woman, two teenagers and three children were done to death in this horrible manner. The killer would render his victims unconscious and then put a plastic bag over their heads, watching as they slowly stifled . . .

"Ugh!" Beth threw the paper down with a shudder. Honestly, the man was repulsive. Fancy keeping something like that all this time! Her brief glance told her that the rest of the cuttings seemed as bad. They were more newspaper accounts of killings and horror.

Footsteps passed the door and the voices of arriving SAPS reached her. She hadn't time to think about what she wanted to do with her find, or if it was important. If Baa-Baa had gone to the trouble of hiding the cuttings they probably were – to him. But to anyone else?

Quickly, she tried to press the book back into its cavity, hoping that the masking tape would hold a second time. She searched for the fallen pin and stuck it in the centre of the top of the planner to keep it up. There didn't seem to be a tell-tale bulge.

Footsteps paused outside the boiler-room door. Beth saw the old *Evening Standard* still lying on the desk.

"Damn!" She shoved it into the middle drawer and slammed it shut.

Grabbing the keys, she made for the door. She didn't know the meaning of her find but instinctively felt it had to be kept secret until she could shed some light on it.

Paula Barton began to open the door and they nearly collided.

"Ah! The keys, Beth, clever girl!" said Paula,

sidestepping a little. "Everything OK?" She nodded towards the interior of the room.

"I suppose so," Beth pulled a face. "Not much to see, not now, anyway. Did you ever see it . . . before?" She was curious to know if Paula had been aware of Baa-Baa's pictorial taste.

Paula hesitated, mirroring Beth's grimace. "Actually, only fleetingly. I kept out. He always locked it, as you know." Her eyes looked over Beth's shoulders, registering the stripped walls.

"The police seem to have done a good job. Thanks for getting the keys – I must get upstairs quickly. So much correspondence before I can get to rehearsal. See you, Beth!" and she turned and left. Beth went in search of her scene gang, closing the boiler-room door firmly behind her with a sense of relief.

There was a good turn-out of SAPS. The real-life drama at The Tree brought them together determined to make their show one of the Tolford Festival highlights. That Friday the theatre positively hummed with life.

Toby and Sam made more blood. Gary was busy with his lighting plot and no one saw him much that day. Jo's father brought her to The Tree in his battered old van. She couldn't manage all the costumes on her bike. Beth saw her stagger in with her arms full, followed by two willing helpers.

Rob started the rehearsal to get it all going before

Paula would be free from her office duties. She had a room off the circle, next to the lighting box.

Beth ran backwards and forwards from stage to scene dock, answering questions and making more lists with the familiar feeling of having wings on her feet, a feeling she always got at this stage of a play.

I'm happy, she thought, surprised.

As she belted up the stage stairs for the hundredth time someone called her name.

"Cheryl!" Beth said. "You've come back!"

"It took a bit of doing, but I won in the end." Cheryl's face was flushed and excited. "Have they started?"

"Quick! You'll be wanted soon. End of Act One's coming up. You haven't been missed."

Cheryl didn't notice the slight edge in her voice.

"Brilliant!" She passed her and disappeared.

Thinking that this was probably a battle Cheryl's parents would never win, Beth went up too.

Tracy Catchpole sat in the prompt corner, a script on her knees. Beth caught a glimpse of Fiona's face in the circle, watching. Toby was on stage with Antonia. It was the moment when Bella, then plain Ellen, was being persuaded by her lover to elope with him to London. She could see Cheryl waiting in the wings to interrupt them. Looking at her eager, alert face, Beth had to remind herself that there was another side to Cheryl, one she was beginning to recognize. Under her fragile little-girl pose she sensed a will of iron, seldom glimpsed but always at work – Cheryl making sure she got what she wanted, no matter what.

Beth realized with a slight start that she disliked Cheryl.

Her eyes switched to Toby. Could Cheryl wheedle him into doing something she wouldn't do for herself, like murder? Did he doctor the paint for her? Was there something in what Gary had said in the boiler room, or was he just trying to make her suspect Toby to take notice away from himself? That half-hearted pass at her suggested as much.

Beth felt bleak. What she would have thought unthinkable a week ago was very thinkable now. Each of her friends had suddenly grown two faces: the face she had always known and felt safe with and another face, only dimly seen, that peered out of the darkness at her, threatening and strange.

Toby was performing one of his big speeches on stage – rather well, Beth thought. His movements were controlled; he didn't wander about as he spoke but delivered his lines confidently and with clarity. She wondered how the make-up department would ever get his shock of unruly hair to look even vaguely Victorian.

Beth knew she had to try to have it out with him if she was ever to have any peace of mind. She thought she'd try to grab him after his brief appearance in Act Two. As she checked the prop table for the Act Two props she determined to find out if he really was hiding anything and, if she could, where she stood with him.

She was passing through the green room when the costume-room door opened and Jo came out.

"Got a mo?" she called. The unusual sound of merry chatter followed her out.

"What's going on in there, Jo? Parrots Anonymous?"

Jo didn't grin, she looked concerned. "There's an . . . odd smell in here," she said hesitantly.

"Smell? Could be someone isn't using—"

"Not that kind of smell. Come and see." Beth followed her back in.

"Hi!" She waved to Jo's two helpers. "My, it's roomy in here!" They laughed.

"Just sniff," Jo said. Beth did. She had smelt this before.

"Cleaning fluid?" she asked tentatively.

"No, silly! Stephanotis!"

"You're joking!" Beth looked at her.

"It's my favourite. I always get it."

"Then it's followed you here, with everything else, from home."

Jo looked relieved. "That could be it, but it's so strong and I'm only using the talc at the moment."

"Perhaps Beanie got to it and sprinkled it about.

It's pure coincidence." Beth couldn't cope with the thought of Bella Gardoni at this point, or her ghost. Nor could she remember the precise moment when she had smelled that perfume before.

"By all that's holy, what's that?" she exclaimed as the sound of what could only be described as a rabble filled the green room next door.

Jo's helpers rose as one. "Coffee break," they said in chorus and squeezed their way to the door.

The kettle was on and the room vibrated to the combined voices of SAPS. Scene dock SAPS poured in and the noise level rose. Beth and Jo joined the mob, but there were no mugs left by the time they got near the coffee. It was rare for so many SAPS to be there at once.

"I'll get us some," Beth offered, remembering the mugs in the boiler room. Not that I want to enter that beastly place again, she thought as she ran down the passage.

She scooped up three of the dirty mugs from the worktop, keeping her eyes away from the walls and their lewd, empty spaces. Then she noticed the desk. There was something different about it. The middle drawer was open.

Putting down the mugs again, she stared at it. Only the paperclip stared back at her. The front page of the old *Evening Standard* was gone.

Now, that's odd. Who would want to take that old newspaper? Beth wondered. She was still puzzled as her eyes went to the year-planner on the wall. It looked the same but she put out a hand to feel its cavity. Then she froze. Was that a scream? With all the babble coming from the green-room end of the passage she wasn't sure. It sounded as if it came from the washrooms next door. She was there in a flash.

Fiona stood beside the basins with her eyes tight shut and a thread of blood trickling down the side of her cheek. Her cotton jumper lay in a heap against a cubicle door. It looked as if it had been thrown there. She was taking a deep breath as if she meant to scream again.

"Fiona!" Beth's exclamation stopped her and she opened her eyes.

"Oh, Beth!" It was a gasp of sheer terror. "I've had the most terrible warning!"

"Warning?" Beth could only echo her.

Fiona turned to the long mirror. "Oh, look at my face! Look at my face!" She seemed hysterical.

Beth went to her, pulled her round and peered at the line of blood. It was a long scratch, not very deep.

"Come on," she said, trying to sound matter-of-fact. "You've only scratched yourself. The make-up'll cover it."

"No! You don't understand. Look!" With a

gesture of high drama Fiona held out her hand to Beth. A comical little felt frog lay on her outstretched palm.

Beth found herself agreeing with Fiona. She didn't understand. Irritation with the silly girl began to mount.

"It's Nostradamus," Fiona said as if that explained everything.

"Now I've heard it all," said Beth, feeling slightly hysterical in her turn.

"No. Look at his poor face." Fiona thrust the little frog towards her and Beth stared at it. She saw that three dressmaking pins had been thrust deeply into the little piece of felt that was its face.

"He's my lucky mascot. He goes everywhere with me. And now look at my face!" This speech ended in a wail and Fiona's startling blue eyes began to fill with tears. "It's the most terrible warning! Something frightful's going to happen," she said, and began to sob.

Beth's kind heart quenched her irritation and she put her arms round Fiona's shaking shoulders. The girl was genuinely upset.

"Now," she said gently, "let's be sensible about this. Tell me what really happened. How did you scratch your face?"

Fiona gulped. "At the break," she began more calmly, "I popped in here to go to the loo and give my hair a comb. I was feeling a bit chilly so I took my pullover out of my bag to put it on. Then I saw what had happened to Nostradamus, and – Beth," she clutched her arm, "I got this awful feeling and went cold all over." She shuddered.

"So you put your jumper on." Beth tried to keep her to the facts.

"As I got it over my head I felt this searing pain, almost in my eye. I jerked the jumper off again and threw it down. It's over there," Fiona pointed.

Beth went and picked the jumper up. It didn't take long to find that three pins had been inserted into the neckline, pointing inwards. Fiona's thick hair must have deflected two of them, but the third had found its mark.

"Fiona," she looked at the younger girl seriously, "you don't really believe in all this psychic stuff, do you? This has been done by someone to hurt you, not by a ghost or anything like that. If it's a warning it's to make you stop all this nonsense – it's to poke fun at you."

Beth could tell she wasn't getting through to her. Maybe someone else does take it all seriously, she thought suddenly.

"Did you hold your seance?" she asked.

"Well, no. The others thought we ought to wait until after the funeral, and we haven't had time yet."

Beth heard Sam's voice again: "She's going to ask him who did it." Lots of people had heard him say that. Was there someone who did not want her to try it, who believed she could get an answer from the dead Baa-Baa? If Sam was the guilty person he might be trying to get in with Fiona just to put her off her psychic stroke. Beth felt he took Fiona's powers seriously enough.

She grappled with this idea. It didn't really seem like Sam's scene – not pins. Then in her mind's eye she saw Jo's long fingers slipping pins into Bella's costumes. Jo again. She shook herself. Other people had access to pins, for God's sake. Somehow she had to find out if Sam had told Jo about the blood plot. She had said she didn't know.

They were waiting for the mugs. Beth had to go.

Fiona suddenly grabbed her wrist and stared into her face. Beth, not used to meeting a stare of such intensity, felt a shiver begin somewhere near her neck. Really, there was something creepy about this girl, silly or not.

"Beth!" Fiona was whispering urgently. "Your aura looks dreadful, it really does. You have to be careful." She gave a little gasp and shut her eyes for a second. Beth felt powerless to pull away from her. The shiver moved up to the base of her scalp. Fiona's eyes opened again and she went on in the same soft, urgent whisper. "You have to be careful, Beth. You're in the most ghastly danger."

"Oh, you stupid little cow!" Beth exploded. "You really are too much! Just stop it. SAPS doesn't need your brand of mumbo-jumbo. It's got its own problems, and you can leave me out of it too."

She turned on her heel, grabbing the mugs as she went. "It's probably far too late for these now," she muttered as she stamped up the passage. "Personally, I'd like to stick pins all over her! Little drama-seeking troublemaker!"

12

Beth didn't get Toby alone until much later in the afternoon. Many SAPS had gone home and work went on with the remaining hard core of people. Toby's acting was over for the day when he and Beth found themselves finishing some elaborately draped curtaining on a window flat. They were alone in the scene dock.

They worked in silence for a bit, Toby quiet and preoccupied and Beth unsure how to begin. At last she took the plunge.

"I went into Baa-Baa's boiler room this morning," she said in a neutral tone of voice. "To look for keys."

Toby had a mouth full of pins. "Hummm," he said.

"What was it like when you saw it?"

"Hmmwhamm?"

"Toby, please, I need you." Beth hoped a direct appeal would do the trick. When there was no reply she went on doggedly.

"When did you see inside the boiler room?" She tried a different question.

Toby sighed as if it was all too boring, but he put the pins down.

"Oh, I forget . . . perhaps two years ago. And yes, it was covered with filthy pictures, like I said." He stabbed a pin into the velvet and didn't look at her, keeping his voice as neutral as hers. "Why?"

"I saw an old newspaper with a scrapbook there. The police hadn't spotted them. The paper's headline was a report of the trial of a murderer called the Bag Killer. The paper was five years old." Beth paused. "When I had to go back in there for some mugs just now, it had gone."

"And the scrapbook?"

"It was there." Beth thought she wouldn't tell him where it was.

Toby shrugged. "It's probably full of reporters' accounts of other killers and the like. There were at least two scrapbooks full when I was there. He was obsessed." Toby's voice thickened with disgust.

"Just lying about?"

"Well, sort of. In drawers and that." Toby was non-committal.

No hidey-hole then. Beth struggled to remember Toby two years younger – a pale, skinny boy, growing far too fast. She hadn't liked him much. He was always getting into some sort of trouble. She searched her memory. Was it shoplifting or under-age drinking? She couldn't recall.

Gary's voice came back to her. "He's got a record." Had it *really* got that bad? Beth pushed the thought away firmly. That adolescent boy was nothing like this attractive young man who could talk himself out of any corner and who was looking at her now with cornflower-blue eyes.

"Why were you there, Toby? You were a very junior SAP then. Why did you have the dubious privilege?" Nothing ventured, nothing gained. Go straight for it, girl, she thought.

"Oh, leave it, Beth! It was ages ago." Toby reached for the pins again. He sounded irritated.

"Toby, it's not the time for secrets." To her relief, Beth began to feel cross. Anything was better than the ache she'd begun to hate. "I'm doing my best to piece all this horrible business together because I can't stand what it's doing to SAPS and I'll never get anywhere near it if there are secrets. You can't want to go on for ever carrying this murder around inside you, not knowing who or why, poisoning your relationships. Look what it's doing to us!"

"Us?" Toby straightened up and looked at her.

"Nobody's really talking to anyone any more:

Cheryl, Sam, Gary – even Jo. And . . ." Beth paused and took a deep breath, "you and me," she ended flatly.

Toby was silent.

She stopped to take another breath and went on more calmly.

"Yes, you and me. We used to be friends, remember? We used to have fun . . ." To her horror her voice threatened to shake. She went on, gathering firmness. "Do you honestly think I'm capable of keeping quiet about your bloody prank for ever? Baa-Baa was *murdered*, for God's sake! I shall be in enough trouble as it is hiding what I know from the police. I don't want a murderer to go free any more than they do but I can't believe that any one of my friends is a killer. I'm trying to get at the truth!"

Her eyes began to fill with unwanted tears. "Please, Toby, tell me if there's anything I should know. Did he have something on you too? Gary seemed to hint that he did."

Toby flared up. "Gary!" He sounded contemptuous. "He's just . . ."

"Jealous?" Beth completed his unfinished sentence. "You must admit, you're as vulnerable as everybody else, if only on Cheryl's behalf."

For the first time Toby turned and really looked at Beth. It was a troubled look and for a moment the old Toby she knew was in it.

"OK." He sighed deeply and flung the pins back in the tin. "There was a time when the cash from the box office spent the night in Mr Lamb's room at the end of a show, right? They don't do it now. My dad had a lot to do with The Tree at that time and I kicked about here nearly every day. I had nothing else to do, and I liked it anyway.

"One Sunday after some show or other had come and gone I was in here while Dad's electricians were putting in the motor for the new stage trap. Mr Lamb's door wasn't locked – it should have been when the money was there but he was always slack about it – and I went into his room because I was bored."

The vision of a bored, lonely adolescent flitted into Beth's mind. She remembered him now. Privileged because he was the son of The Tree's benefactor, who was also rich, he always seemed to have anything he wanted, from the latest piece of electronic gadgetry to the best designer trainers. But he had no circle of friends then; he tried to hang out with the older SAPS, who didn't want him, and was a real show-off to his contemporaries. Let's face it, Beth mused, he wasn't liked.

"There was lots to look at, as you can imagine. I'd been in before, poking about." Toby smiled without humour. "I found the cash box in his desk and picked it up, giving it a good shake – and he came in. End of story."

"He thought you were going to steal it?"

"Well, he didn't think I was going to eat it. I probably would have taken the money if I could have got at it – I don't know. Things I did then didn't make a lot of sense always."

"Oh, Toby!" Beth's sympathy rose. "I suppose he told your dad?"

"That's just it." Toby spoke bitterly. "He didn't. He always threatened to, of course, and when you're a kid you believe that. I was scared stiff. I'd got into so much trouble as it was. I knew that if Dad heard about it he'd never believe that I wouldn't have taken it. He didn't like me much."

"Don't be daft, he's your dad." In Beth's experience parents liked their children.

"Beth," Toby said quietly, "Dad drove my mother into that tree. He was hardly hurt at all. He felt – feels – so guilty."

Beth noticed the present tense and felt chilled.

"Still?"

"Still. Only it's almost worse now he's keen on Paula."

"Worse?"

"I've never told anyone this, so you've got to swear to keep it to yourself."

"I swear, Toby. You're important to me, you know." But he wasn't really listening. He was struggling to find the right words for what he had to tell her.

"Last summer I had a bit of a 'thing' for Paula."

Beth tried to lighten things. "You and whose army?" she teased him gently. He didn't smile back.

"She seemed so – perfect. Dad was getting to know her too. He'd been impressed at her interview. I remember how he described her. Things are never right between Dad and me, ever. We just live together, we don't talk." Toby paused. "I mean," he carried on, "you would think we could at least share our joint interest in The Tree, wouldn't you? But no. Somehow I get the distinct impression that it would be better if I kept off the subject of Paula and even The Tree when he's around. It's as if he's jealous of all the time I spend around Paula – as if I was some sort of threat to him!

"All the time I was falling a bit in love with her and took to writing her poems. For God's sake don't breathe any of this!"

Beth's mind had gone into overdrive. This was a can of worms she hadn't dreamed existed. That Toby had been half in love with Paula didn't shock her – most of SAPS, girls and boys, got a crush on her at one time or another. But his dad's reaction – that was beyond her. She felt so sorry for him. He was living in an emotional minefield.

"Well, I wrote these poems in between entrances during the last production. They were quite terrible really, and I had no intention of anyone reading them, but I did mean every single word. Baa-Baa came upon them in the dressing room one careless moment and let me know he had them. He . . . flaunted them at me!"

"So," said Beth, "he said he'd show them to Paula. He wanted more power over you. The old threat of the money box was out of date."

"Yes, the old threat was getting stale. But no, not Paula – much worse. Dad. If Dad saw them I would have had to leave home. I guessed Dad was considering marrying Paula. He was having trouble with the old guilt over that too. Baa-Baa was just waiting to use those poems. The hell was, I never knew when. He would have done it. Oh, Beth, I hated him!"

Instinctively, Beth put her arm round his waist.

"Poor old you," she said softly, thinking as she did so, don't let it be you, Toby. Please, not you.

Toby didn't draw away, he turned and they hugged each other, Beth's face pressed against the middle of his T-shirt.

"You're gold dust, you know?" he told her.

They parted awkwardly and Toby pulled her hair gently. "What now, Sherlock?"

Beth sighed. "OK, Watson. Back to basics, in this case the blood. What did you all do *after* the bucket had been taken up to the gantry?" Beth was back on track and her heart should have been lighter by kilos, but after what Toby had told her it wasn't.

"Sam went out and got us burgers from Mac's and we sat in the stalls and watched the rehearsal. Oh, we kept an eye on Cheryl. You know what she's like, and she had a job to do."

"Otherwise all was normal?"

"Well, yes. Paula took the prompt book in the corner, leaving Rob to cope out front as no one knew their lines and she was going spare. She didn't let them read, she just put them through agony. It was quite painful, actually." Toby grinned for the first time.

"I bet." Beth chuckled. "She's not usually so hard on them. Her headache must have got to her. So, when did she call a halt?"

"Just after half past nine. We kicked about a bit and pretended to be getting ready to go while everyone packed up."

"Was Jo around, d'you know?"

"She might have been; I didn't see her. We agreed we'd go up the gantry steps one after the other with Cheryl last as she had to tape up her drawing when no one was about."

"How did she manage to disappear?"

"She said she hid in the loos."

So, Beth thought quickly. The bucket was in place during the last bit of the rehearsal. When it was over the boys went up to the gantry one by one to avoid notice. Any one of them could have slipped the weight in the paint then under the pretext of giving it a stir. It's dark up there and they could have done it easily. Cheryl probably didn't as she was preoccupied with the drawing and the last to go up. That still doesn't leave out Jo. Seeing Toby go up with the bucket she could have slipped up there next before the others got assembled. I really don't think I'm up to this!

"Toby," she said aloud, "does anyone know who was last out of the theatre?"

"Cheryl may know as the loos are near the scene dock."

"I'll ask her. Of course," she added, thinking aloud, "the field's wide open still."

Toby picked up the pins and Beth gathered a handful of velvet to drape it over the flat. They worked in silence for a while, deep in their own thoughts.

Little by little the actors trickled past them on their way home. Fiona and a group of younger SAPs came through in a body. Beth noticed that although she looked pale she seemed to have recovered from her brush with the pins and wore her long hair over the scratched side of her face. She didn't look at Beth.

Cheryl and Sam were the last of the leading actors to come out. It had been a long day.

"Paula's closeted with that Detective Chief Inspector in her office," announced Cheryl. "He's been shown round every corner of The Tree yet again."

The news of a police presence sobered them.

Beth watched Toby's face. It didn't tell her anything.

The three boys and Cheryl had been grilled more than once. They'd stuck to their agreed story. They had made the blood, left it in the scene dock and not seen it again. They hadn't noticed that it was missing because they knew Beth always tidied up before going home. On the question of Mr Lamb having enemies, they were reserved. Yes, he wasn't popular, but as far as they knew nobody had a special grudge. It was a mystery.

Sam recovered first.

"He hasn't got anyone to 'help him with his inquiries' yet," he said, zipping up his anorak with a flourish. "Fiona says he hasn't got a strong enough aura."

"If I hear that word 'aura' again . . ." Beth left the sentence hanging on the air.

"So it's Fiona now, young Sam?" Toby ribbed him. "We thought you rather fancied someone else."

"Has anyone seen anything of Gary?" Beth broke in hastily. She wasn't sure if Toby had Jo in mind and if so she didn't want it bandied about behind her back.

"He's gone," said Cheryl. "Having a policeman in his precious lighting box was too much for him," she giggled. "I know what he's like!"

"Too true!" It slipped out before Beth could help it.

"What's that supposed to mean?" Cheryl bridled.

Beth watched her sidle up to Toby and take his arm. She was looking at Beth. It was an obvious 'he's mine' gesture.

Is that for protection? Does she imagine I'm going to attack her? Beth's thoughts were grim.

But quick as a flash Cheryl changed tack. She turned on Sam, who was still fiddling with his zip.

"And you needn't think zipping yourself up like a banana will hide it, Sam," she said with a slightly vicious grin.

Toby and Beth stared at him. Sam clutched his breast. Cheryl pounced and struggled to reach the zip flap.

"Get off!" Sam shoved her.

"Go on, show us, Sam," Beth turned on her charm. Anything to lighten the atmosphere. It worked.

"Oh, I know you'll laugh . . ." Sam slowly undid his zip and pulled out a leather thong with a piece of crystal hanging from it. "It's a piece of rough agate," he said sheepishly.

The others looked blank.

"It helps to prosper a career and protect one from danger." Sam tried to sound matter-of-fact.

"Fiona says," said Toby, and Cheryl hooted with laughter.

"And," Sam said, looking hurt, "it brings sympathy to the wearer – or it should."

Beth picked up her basket. "I'll give you lots of sympathy, Sam," she said. She couldn't help smiling at him, he was such a clown. "I'll buy you a Coke. Come on, let's go eat. I fancy a plate of Mac's egg and chips. And Cheryl, as we go, I need to know something."

"Tell me," Beth spoke urgently to make Cheryl listen. "You went to hide in the loos last Saturday evening, right?"

"Yeah?" Cheryl wasn't sure how much Beth knew.

"Toby said," Beth reassured her. "And I need to know everything you heard while you were waiting for the rest to leave, OK?"

"Well," Cheryl shrugged as she thought back. "It was dead boring. I sat on a seat with the door shut at first and then I opened it when I thought it was safe. I could hear feet going by and voices. Toni paid a quick visit to comb her hair – she was going out with Rob for a drink."

"Can you remember who was the last voice you heard?"

"I think it was Paula's. She was opening and shutting the doors to see if everyone was out as she always does on her way down the passage. Baa-Baa must have come out of his door at the time to begin locking up, because I heard him call her name."

"Did you hear what they said?"

"Not really. He said he'd got something of hers, I think."

"Oh?"

"Yeah, I remember . . . he said something about finding whatever it was somewhere. Could have been his boiler room . . . or the scene dock . . . I don't know where."

"And then what did she say?"

"Come to think of it, I didn't hear her say very much. But I knew she was there because Baa-Baa was talking to her, or to someone. But it was very muffled."

"Was that everything?"

"Yeah. Then she went and I heard Baa-Baa's footsteps go past on his last round, circle first and then stage door and that, so I flew up the stairs, taped the drawing and got up the gantry just as he came into the auditorium. Whew! Was my heart beating!"

I must have got the whole picture by now, thought Beth. There were no surprises about Paula being the last to leave the theatre. Apart from Baa-Baa she usually was.

I don't feel any wiser though, she thought glumly. It's like some blooming great jigsaw puzzle scattered over my mind! I'll have to put it all down on paper, then perhaps I'll see some sort of pattern to it.

"Race you! I can taste those chips!" Cheryl, fair hair streaming, sprinted the last few metres to Mac-Henry's glass door and the boys crowded in after her, pushing and shoving.

Beth followed more slowly. She could feel a deep gulf beginning to divide her from the others. She would have given anything she possessed to be able to talk it through with someone, but who?

She thought longingly of Paula and her offer of friendship. She could still do that as long as she could be sure Paula wouldn't suddenly become all 'grown-up' and dash off to the police. That was the trouble – she might. Beth went through the café doors and saw the others already queueing at the counter.

Oh well, she shrugged inwardly as she joined them, as least she's there if I get desperate.

13

The week before the first night of *Bella* was fraught. The combined dance and ballet schools of Tolford Regis were having a show the week after SAPS. They needed to rehearse on the stage so Paula had to squeeze rehearsals into whatever space she could find during the times when the stage was banned to them. The scene dock was getting so full it was difficult to move in it, and Jo collared whoever she could and clapped costumes on wherever she found them.

Beth's days were full to bursting and she cycled home each evening tired out. Productions were always hard work but this time her fatigue was different. There were moments when all her energy threatened to fail her.

What's the matter with me? she wondered, as she dragged herself upstairs on the Wednesday before the show. The dress rehearsal's not until Sunday and I feel exhausted now.

Her mother brought her up a cup of chocolate, just like she did when Beth was little, and sat on the edge of her bed.

"Are you eating properly, Beth?" she asked. "I know you and productions. One choc bar and a plate of chips is not enough."

Beth smiled. Her mother's standard question was strangely comforting. It was like a lighthouse shining in the uncharted sea she felt herself to be sailing. It was almost as if she was living two lives at the same time: one exciting and familiar, full of the hurly-burly of theatre and company life, and the other a bleak and dangerous landscape – a country where even familiar things and people assumed shapes she did not recognize.

There was Toby, with his troubled past, driven and tormented by pressures she could barely understand under the dark shadow of his father.

Cheryl, wilful and explosive, who, perhaps without knowing it herself, would manipulate any situation to get what she wanted, especially if her desires were about to be thwarted.

Gary, intense and private, revealing himself to be fiercely possessive and full of deep feelings of jealousy. His high intelligence set him a little apart anyway, but now he seemed positively withdrawn.

Sam, an emotional firecracker, needing to be top but fearing he was bottom. Unable to take humiliation of any kind, much less the sort that Baa-Baa had dished out.

Jo, friend of many years, hiding a deep scar from the world. Beth felt that she didn't really know her, after all.

The list read like the cast list of a popular melodrama, not a description of her closest friends. Would they ever be the same carefree group after this? She doubted it.

Her mother smoothed Beth's hair and touched her cheek. "Is everything OK?"

Beth longed to say "No, everything's dreadful. I don't know who anybody is any more," but she took a sip of chocolate and nodded at her mother over the rim of the cup.

Jan Greene sighed. She knew when to push her daughter and when to let her go. Things were clearly not OK. How could they be? she thought. Let them all get this show over and then we'll see . . .

She patted Beth's shoulder and stood up.

"Paula's going to let me work the trap tomorrow," Beth told her, determined to sound positive.

"Good, love. Mind you don't fall into it, then!" And they both laughed.

*   *   *

"It's so simple," Paula said. "Look." She was standing behind Beth in the prompt corner, facing the mechanism that worked the trap door in the stage.

"First you have to turn on the switch and then all you do is pull that lever and – hey presto!" She did so.

Almost silently a part of the stage floor, about two metres square, dropped away and came to a halt about two metres down. It was downstage centre, directly behind the old orchestra pit. It could be reached from below stage via the passage off the green room.

"Now, Beth," Paula went on seriously, "your job will be to make sure someone is under the stage by the trap ready to fling the mattresses on it. Two people probably. Toni is not to be allowed to fall without them, understand? We'll go through it first a few times without her so you'll get the timing. Right?"

"Right," Beth said. Heavens! she thought. What a responsibility. But she also thought, Jo'll be good, and Tracy's keen – they'll do it. I've got to stick to the mechanism up here.

On stage an ageing Bella was having a row with her cooling lover. The quarrel took the actors, Antonia and Sam, upstage above the trap. Completely absorbed by her passion Bella doesn't see the trap opening behind her. When she turns away in despair after her lover has left her she falls into it.

In the drama Bella falls onto a pair of antlers, their horns sharpened, slipped on to the trap floor by the murderer. She dies, covered with blood, after being impaled on them.

The girls had to put the mattresses in place during the moments of the play just before Bella turns around to fall into the trap. To her relief Beth discovered that there was enough time to get them there safely.

Antonia prepared to do her first fall, the two girls stood, mattresses at the ready, and Beth had her hand poised over the trap lever. She pulled it and with a soft sigh the trap responded. Antonia swivelled round, screamed and fell.

Immediately another scream filled the auditorium. Fiona McLaren was up in the circle and was now hanging over the edge of the balcony, waving her arms, a white face in a halo of shadowy hair.

"Oh lord! It's the resident gloom prophet again," muttered Beth as Fiona's shrill voice reached her in her corner of the stage. "Doesn't she ever get tired?"

"It's Bella!" she cried as every face turned to look at her. "She isn't happy – she's trying to tell us!"

Paula, startled at this interruption, stared up at her. "What are you talking about, Fiona?" She sounded irritated too.

"Oh, Paula!" There was high drama in Fiona's

voice. "I can smell her perfume. It's stephanotis, I know it is. It's all over the circle. It's because of the death in her theatre, I know it is. Another violent death that will never be solved. She's trying to tell us. Nostradamus is trying to tell us. I just know!"

"You don't know anything of the sort, Fiona," Paula shouted. "You have totally interrupted an important moment in the rehearsal. Come down here at once and stop being such an idiot!"

"But . . . the scent . . ." Fiona could see now that Paula looked really angry. "Honestly, Paula . . ." A faint whiff of some flowery smell floated down to the stalls.

"I know it's late in the day, Fiona," Paula spoke with deadly control, "but your part isn't so big that I couldn't replace you now. Come down at once."

That's telling her! By the side of the stage Beth grinned. Fiona disappeared.

"OK, Sam, take it from where Bella slaps your face." Sam groaned and clutched his head. Paula took no notice. "Beth, stand by." The rehearsal went on.

The last act of the play drew to a close. Antonia, in Bella's dying words, gasped out her last breath and Paula shouted to Beth, "Curtain!"

She unhitched the rope and began to turn the handle that drew the heavy curtains shut. Antonia got to her feet and in a babble of chatter they waited for Paula to begin to give them their notes.

Beth wound the curtain open again, and as she did so she felt a cold shiver begin at her ankles and work its way slowly up her spine until it made her scalp tingle.

I know what it is, she told herself. It's the fact that we're all involved with the story of a murder that happened here about a hundred years ago. We're doing it again on the same stage in the same theatre. I happen to be standing almost on the exact spot where another murder happened, was it only ten days ago? No wonder I feel spooked. I don't need Bella's ghost to tell me – I know!

Paula was giving everybody the countdown time-table. The following day, Friday, they had the stage for only half the day. Saturday morning the stage crew needed it to begin to set up, and Gary and his team had to begin to shift and set the lights. In the afternoon Jo had her dress parade and after that there'd be a rehearsal. Sunday morning was a technical run when all the music and lighting cues were run through and the stage crew rehearsed their scene changes (there were three big ones), followed by a full dress rehearsal starting at two o'clock. Monday was *Bella*'s first night.

The realization that countdown had begun had its usual rather sobering effect on everyone. Posters for *Bella* had been dotted around Tolford for the last two weeks. The strong black-and-white image of a Victorian beauty now held a personal significance for every SAP. They were all part of it. Rumours of good ticket sales sent a thrill of anticipation down every neck. They were going to do well.

For the first time Mr Lamb's death began to take a back seat.

Friday evening arrived and the late rehearsal was over. Toby and one or two scene painters were still cleaning out their brushes in the washrooms. Jo had left earlier. Most of the costumes were ready to be moved into the dressing rooms. They were hanging in Jo's tiny room on every possible piece of furniture and hook. It looked like some old pawn shop from the last decade. Beth, ready to go home, poked her nose round Jo's door. Seeing that her bag was gone, she carried on into the passage. Each door had a small fanlight above it and Beth saw that the light in the star dressing room was on.

I might catch Jo, she thought, pushing the door open. The idea that Jo might just be the person to talk to had been growing in her mind. After all, if Jo hadn't been part of the 'plot' and didn't know anything about it as she claimed, then she wasn't really involved. If she was lying and Beth began to talk about it, she might find herself unable to keep the secret. Either way, Beth would know.

An overpowering smell rushed out to meet her. It was so strong it made her eyes water. Stephanotis?

Then Beth realized that the dress rail wasn't empty. Bella Gardoni's ballgown was hanging on it. Down the front of the dress, from its beautiful lace collar, over the rich velvet bodice and full skirt, spread a dark red stain. A pool had gathered under the hemline on the dressing-room floor.

She walked slowly forward and touched it.

"It's wet!" she gasped, looking at the red marks on her fingers.

She fled from the room and slammed the door behind her.

"What on earth's going on?" she said aloud.

Paula came into the passage rattling her keys. "Everybody out!" she called, pausing when she saw Beth. "Hey, you look as if you've seen a ghost!" She spoke merrily, then stopped abruptly when she saw Beth's face.

Beth opened the door to the star dressing room. "What d'you make of that?" she asked.

Stephanotis leaked into the passage and spread quickly.

Paula went in.

"Phew, what a stink!" This from an outraged SAP, standing outside the washrooms waving his brushes like a fan.

Toby joined him. "Beth," he joked, "time you changed your perfume . . . that's awful!"

All of them stared at the stained dress on the rail. Then Paula spoke, realizing what they must be dreading. "It's only paint, of course."

"It's not Bella's death-scene dress, it's her ball-gown." Beth began to feel angry. How could anyone do this to Jo? Then the thought quickly followed, could Jo do this to one of her costumes if she needed to throw people off the scent? Oh, that blasted scent again! It *would* be her favourite and she knows where to get it! Oh, Jo!

"She'll space out!" Toby said as he examined the front of the dress. "She'll have to find something to get it off."

"I'll take it home with me now," Paula began to take the dress off the hanger. "Toby, wipe the floor, there's a dear. I'll get the worst off before Jo sees it. Then clear out everybody and get some rest. Tomorrow's a long day."

The scene painters waltzed down the passage together making ghostly noises and spooky gestures. "See you in the graveyard!" one shouted as they disappeared into the scene dock.

Beth and Toby moved off too and Paula continued locking up.

As she paused to pick up her basket Beth said, "It can't really be Bella, can it, Toby? It's the third time we've smelled her perfume. Once in Jo's room, once in the circle and now here."

He didn't answer at once. "Theatres are odd

171

places, full of old superstitions and such." He sounded thoughtful. "There's been dramatic doings here, God knows, and we're acting out Bella's story . . . but I'd rather think it was the daft Fiona at work, wouldn't you?"

Beth agreed with that. What a day! She had felt better since her talk with Toby. It had cleared the air a little and some of their old camaraderie had returned.

They had left the scene dock and were standing beside Beth's bicycle. The day had been blisteringly hot but they hadn't noticed. Inside The Tree the temperature always seemed the same, summer or winter, and one tended to lose touch with reality after a long day inside. Normal life ceased as soon as they entered. It had always been like that.

Beth answered him. "Yes, I would, but it's hard to believe that even Fiona would be so . . . mischievous." She strapped on her basket.

The door of the scene dock clanged shut. Paula had come out and was locking it from the outside.

Beth thought she saw the muscles of Toby's jaw tighten as she turned towards them. She sighed inwardly.

"I'll walk with you, Toby," Paula called. "I'm coming to your house for supper." As well as her own bag she carried Bella's stained costume in a plastic carrier.

"'Bye, Beth!" said Toby, and he gave her arm a squeeze.

Beth guided her bike over the rough ground of the car park towards the high street. "'Bye, both!" she said over her shoulder as she passed them. Then she turned the corner and began to pedal northwards. Toby's fingers pressing on her arm had made her glow.

At a zebra crossing she stopped while an old lady with a white stick was guided across.

"Beth!"

She turned and saw Mark standing on the pavement beside her. She waved at him.

"I've got my ticket for the last night," he said. "You should all know what you're doing by then!"

"Do you mind!" Beth tried to look indignant, quite hard with one leg each side of a bike.

"Have a drink after the opening?" Beth was preparing to move off now that the old lady was safely on the pavement.

"Er . . . think that's OK. Can you ring me? 'Byeee!" The cars behind were making her move on. She wobbled as she tried to look behind her but only the top of Mark's ginger head was visible above the traffic.

Drat! He hasn't got my number, she remembered. Well, he'll just have to do some research. She was flattered though. She liked the young policeman. He didn't have Toby's looks, that was true, and she didn't know him very well, but he had a way of making her feel special. A girl could do with a lot of that, she reflected with a smile.

The warm summer breeze lifted her hair from her neck and she began to enjoy the steady movement of her cycle as she wove home through the traffic.

She was nearly at the end of her street when she pulled her thoughts together.

"This isn't getting me anywhere," she said aloud. Her ability to solve the mystery was beginning to seem very doubtful. There were motives in plenty, but as for answers. . . ?

Silently she went on. The play is carrying us all along with its own momentum, like being together in a large boat, she thought. We'll land soon and go our different ways and we'll never put this right. I don't know what to think about the ghost business, but it's creepy. It proves that there's something thoroughly nasty around in The Tree – as if we didn't realize that already.

Her mother's car was parked in the road outside their house. Beth wasn't sure she wanted company.

It was going to be difficult to tell Jo about the dress, but she must. She was glad that Paula had whisked it away before Jo saw it.

She put her bike away.

What I really need now, she thought, is a flash of genuine inspiration.

14

Beth arrived at the scene dock door early on Saturday morning and had to hang around for Rob to come and open up. The scenery was going on to the stage today. It consisted mainly of canvas flats. Some of the flats contained doors, others windows or fireplaces. They would be stacked in the wings waiting for their moment of glory on the stage, where they turned themselves into rooms and streets.

The tall flats were roped together firmly and cleated off. They were made to stand up straight by braces from behind held securely down by heavy stage weights.

One of these weights had been used to kill Mr Lamb.

The work was heavy. The scenery had to be manhandled up from the scene dock below through a long opening at the back of the stage in front of the cyclorama. Large pieces of furniture were taken in through the door in the back wall of the theatre.

Big Steve was much in demand. Nothing was too large or too heavy for him. This was his day. He enjoyed acting, but here he was in his element.

Beth threw herself into it all. She arranged the order of the scenery, carried and shoved with the best of them, answered all the questions thrown at her from SAPS who had just turned up that day to help, and instructed the heavy mob where each flat was to go for which Act.

She had made a resolution. She was going to return to Baa-Baa's boiler room to have a proper look at the scrapbook. The disappearance of the old newspaper bothered her and made her think there was more to discover about Mr Lamb. She realized, with a shiver of anxiety, that she was probably the only person who knew about the hiding place and the scrapbook. If she drew a blank there she was stumped.

Of course there was Cheryl's Auntie Gina, who might be a source of information, but getting her to talk about him could be difficult.

Gary was adding to the confusion. He was moving about, trailing cables and manoeuvring lights into their new positions. The lighting bars that spanned the whole stage from side to side were lowered and in danger of knocking the heads off any unwary scene-shifter. Gary wasn't good at telling others what to do anyway, but this time he was wrapped up in his own thoughts. He went doggedly about it all, needing nobody.

Paula stood in the middle of the stage, keeping a careful watch, quietly moving anyone on if they got stuck, always aware of the fleeting time, and providing a secure framework for their energy to spark in.

Beth surfaced for a second and stood beside her.

"Gary's going to need some help soon," Paula said, "like it or not."

"Yeah," Beth agreed. "When everything's up Steve will be free." She sped away again to make sure her prop table wasn't covered by a leaning curtain.

Paula's ace, she thought. She really thinks of everything.

They took an hour for lunch. Paula insisted they ate sensibly to store up strength for the rest of the day. Some of the younger SAPS were sent out for pies and chips and other edibles. They sat about on the stage and on the stall seats in little groups. Paula was circled by the usual throng of devoted fans.

Beth brought her sandwich over to join Toby

and Sam. Gary was nowhere to be seen. He had taken to eating up in his box – in fact, he seemed to stay up there most of the time now.

"So far so good," she sighed, lowering herself onto a tip-up seat.

To her surprise Toby got up slowly and moved down the line of seats away from her. He didn't look at her or say anything. Beth watched him go – it wasn't very far. Cheryl was sitting on the stage dangling her legs over the edge. Toby went to stand below her, then leaned his elbow on the stage and said something in her ear. She giggled and rubbed her shoulder against him.

Beth blinked. Was that what she thought it was – a snub?

Sam didn't seem to notice anything amiss and Beth pretended not to, either. She ate her lunch without much relish, looking at Toby from time to time. It seemed as if he was making a point of not looking around at her.

I'm getting paranoid, she thought. I'd better go and see if Jo needs any extra help. That reminded her.

"Sam," she turned to him suddenly.

He stopped in mid-chew.

"When Jo got the blood that time, did you tell her what you and the others were going to do?"

"She was spell-bound!" Sam began to giggle but then he saw Beth's face. "I'm having you on.

Honestly, Beth, not a word crossed my lips," he spoke through a mouthful of cheese roll.

"I don't think honesty had a lot to do with it!"

Beth got up. She had a strong feeling that she didn't like Sam, either. Was she going to like anybody by the end of this? Sam was a show-off. He'd say anything if he thought it would make him look big. At the moment he didn't look to Beth like murderer material.

The next thought came at her like an express train and her knees felt weak. Sam may not look like *any*one's idea of a murderer but that's exactly what he was. His hand – and nobody else's – had hurled the bucket, the blood and the weight that killed Mr Lamb.

She went below.

Jo and her helpers had spent the whole morning setting up the dressing rooms in preparation for the dress parade. The costumes were labelled with their character's names and hung in bulging ranks on the dress rails. It was quite a large cast. The star dressing room had five in it – capacity level – and the long room was crammed with everyone else. The rooms were well equipped with lights and full-length mirrors and, best of all, wash basins.

Jo had an absorbed air about her that Beth recognized. All her concentration was focused on the task of getting assorted sized SAPS into their costumes and making sure they fitted. She had everything under control, she didn't need any help.

Beth wished she hadn't asked Sam anything. She'd done it on the spur of the moment and now didn't know where she was. She returned to her stage corner and prepared to use the intercom system to summon the cast one by one.

Starting with the small parts, they made their way on stage to stand in the centre and be scrutinized by Paula and also by Jo, who came up to see how each garment looked from the auditorium.

The intercom went blank.

"Not to fret." Gary dropped a cable and crossed to the prompt corner. Beth fled down the stairs to tell the actors what had happened.

The actors in the long dressing room had all been seen. Beth popped her head round the door of the star dressing room where Antonia, Toby, Cheryl, Sam and Fiona were struggling into various garments.

She found Toby, half dressed, fastening the buttons down the back of Cheryl's dress, while Jo was on her knees working at Bella's hemline. She was in the fated ballgown, which had survived the red paint quite well. Jo had cunningly draped a new swag of lace in the front and it looked very pretty.

"Go on stage when you're ready, all," she said. "The intercom's on the blink but Gary the Wiz is fixing it."

Toby finished Cheryl's buttons and she handed him her necklace to fasten, with a long sideways glance. Her eyelashes brushed his cheek. Neither of them looked at Beth.

"We're on our way," Jo said. She rose and, still holding Bella's hem, she and Antonia moved to the door together. Sam and Fiona followed.

"Can I give you a hand, Toby?" Beth saw him struggling with his cravat.

Cheryl swept past her with her skirts swishing.

Toby turned his back to stare into the mirror. He didn't answer.

"Is anything the matter?" Beth asked him, very puzzled.

"No," Toby said shortly. It was obvious he didn't want to add anything.

Beth went out quietly. The intercom spluttered into action and she made her way slowly back up to the stage. She was very hurt. He and Cheryl were obviously shutting her out, but why?

In twos and threes the cast with the smaller parts got out of their costumes and straggled home. Jo disappeared into her room with a pile of things to complete before the dress rehearsal. The afternoon was slipping into evening and Paula kept her principals for a quiet rehearsal of their major scenes. Rob was on the book and Gary was still up his ladder sliding different-coloured gels into his lights, or up on the gantry fiddling with whatever he could reach. Everything had to be in place for the technical run the following morning.

Unwanted for the first time that day, Beth quietly left them to it and made for the boiler room.

She opened the door and then stood stock still with shock. The room was a mess. Someone had been there and wreaked havoc. There wasn't much to destroy but what there was had been. The desk lay on its side where it had obviously been over-turned violently. Old beer cans and the remaining crockery from the worktop were scattered in pieces all over the room. Worst of all, the walls with their tell-tale remnants had been daubed and splashed with the now infamous red paint. The paint spat-tered everything.

Behind the place where the desk had stood when it was upright, the noticeboard was still intact. It had been given its share of paint, but that was all.

Beth stepped gingerly over to the desk with a pounding heart. There *was* something very wrong at work in The Tree. This looked like the work of someone who was close to cracking up, or close to committing another violent act. Either way it held the threat of danger. No scent of stephanotis this time, only the oily smell of the boiler and a thick odour of dust.

Beth would not be put off. She unpinned the planner and removed the scrapbook. Mr Lamb's hidey-hole had been a good one, she reflected, as she flicked through the pages of clippings.

Toby was right. They all dealt with the same sort of subject. Each cutting related to the discovery of the bodies of people killed by serial murderers, then the killers' subsequent arrests, trial and sentences.

By far the largest and most recent was the sordid and terrible account of the Bag Killer. The cuttings spread over several pages. Pathetic photographs of the victims smiled out at her from smudgy newsprint. The face of the frail old lady touched her deeply, but the three laughing, happy children who had met their deaths so brutally, made her feel sick.

"He's a monster," she heard herself whisper. Then she saw a photograph of the killer's mother as she was going in to hear the jury's verdict on her son. She looked ill. As well she might, thought Beth. Then one of the Bag Killer himself, a man in his mid-thirties with a heavy brow shading an otherwise open and attractive face.

Beth wondered if his mother would ever believe that her son had been capable of doing those dreadful things. And if I was married to him . . . She had turned over another leaf and was looking at a woman's haggard face. Her short blonde hair lay in lank spikes on her forehead. The strain on her face was obvious. She was only twenty-nine, but she looked fifty.

Suddenly, Beth had a strong feeling that she was not alone. The hair on the nape of her neck stirred. She heard the boiler-room door creak and her heart jumped into her mouth. She looked round, feeling guilty for being there, and for some reason scared to death. Who was coming in? No one did.

Stuffing the scrapbook up her sweatshirt front to look at later, she left the room in a hurry.

Outside, Beth glanced up and down the passage nervously. Still no one. Convinced that someone had been looking at her in the boiler room, she opened the swing door into the scene dock. The familiar space, now empty of all *Bella*'s scenery, was dark and quiet.

Beth shivered. Someone was there, in the shadow of the prop gallery, watching her. She knew it. Suddenly her beloved Tree felt hostile and threatening. She could hear Fiona's urgent whisper in her ear, "Danger, Beth! You're in danger!" She turned to go but it was too late. Something came at her, spinning through the darkness. It hit her a glancing blow on her shoulder and smashed against the door behind. As she fled, she saw that it was, incongruously, a plaster bust of Queen Victoria!

Shocked and frightened, Beth ran up the passage, clutching her bruised shoulder. She found Jo, her work spread out in the green room, brewing another cup of coffee and struggling with the bones of a corset. She didn't seem to notice Beth's agitation.

Jo's capable hands were stained with red. Beth stared at them.

"It's the devil to get off," Jo muttered, noticing her look.

Beth drew back. She needed comforting and reassurance, but everything was stained, tainted, spoiled – even Jo. Her common sense told her that Jo couldn't be in two places at once, so she wasn't the one in the scene dock throwing things at her, but had she done the work in the boiler room? Or did all that paint get on her fingers when she daubed Bella's ballgown?

She felt sick. Words began to tumble, unbidden, out of her mouth.

"Someone's just attacked me in the scene dock, Jo, and the boiler room's a mess. It's got red paint all over it." Jo's silence drove her on. "I can't take any more of it. I'm going to the police!"

"Beth, no!" Jo spun round.

Beth knew she didn't mean it. Not yet, anyway. But she couldn't help herself.

"What's going on, Jo?" Her control cracked. "Why shouldn't I go to them? No one's telling me the truth, not even you. You *did* know about the boys' plot. You could have put the weight in the bucket, sprayed stephanotis all round the place, stuck pins in Fiona's frog, daubed Bella's dress to make it look like someone else. I know you couldn't have been in the scene dock just now, but by the colour of your hands you could have wrecked the boiler room. All to make it look like the work of some maniac! You had a motive – you hated Lamb!"

Beth, appalled at what she had said, stopped at last.

"Who's talking about the police?"

Gary came into the green room on his way to Jo's cupboard for a plug. He looked at both girls calmly. "Actually, I was thinking of going there myself."

Jo, her face white, sank into a chair. "If either of you go anywhere near the police, you'll be very, very sorry," she said coldly and quietly.

Beth took it in. No pleading, no reasons, just a bald threat.

Gary said, almost conversationally, "It can't be allowed to go on like this, you know, Jo. I have a good idea who killed the Sheep, and after the show I shall tell them." They were staring at each other, holding each other's eyes defiantly.

Panic seized Beth. She knew there was more to it now than a weight and a bucket of blood. But they didn't. They didn't know about the disappearing newspaper or the bust of Queen Victoria that had hurtled at her with the intention of stunning her, or worse.

She suspected that Gary had been brewing up for something like this. Being alone so much he had been brooding and planning. If he had murdered Lamb, then calling the police would deflect suspicion. If he hadn't he'd bring it all down on the others' heads. Beth forgot for a moment that she had been threatening to do just that herself.

"Look." She tried to keep her voice normal but her shoulder was aching. She rubbed it. "Let's just keep cool. I'm sorry if I lost mine just now." She knew Jo wouldn't forget what she had said about being attacked, but Gary probably hadn't heard.

"The most important thing now is the show. It's nearly opening night. Let's call a truce, eh?"

"OK." *Bella* was top of everyone's list. Gary calmly moved off across the green room. "Truce, but only till after the show." He disappeared into the costume room, leaving Beth and Jo looking at each other bleakly.

"Jo," Beth's voice was full of misery, "I thought you trusted me."

Jo's face didn't change.

"I thought I *could* trust you." She left the unspoken words "but now . . ." hanging in the air.

"Please let's talk this over tonight, at home." Beth was cut to the quick. "You haven't forgotten you're staying with us, have you?" Jo usually spent the night before a dress rehearsal at Beth's, as it wasn't so far for her to cycle. It was part of the ritual and they both enjoyed it.

"Don't worry," Jo turned back to her corset and

gave a final tug. The bone slid into place. "I'll ring my father. He'll come for me."

"Oh, Jo! I couldn't bear it if we weren't friends any more!" This was a cry from Beth's heart. "I know things are rotten. I know I said things to you, but I've been so frightened . . . and you've been so strange."

Rob and Antonia came in before Beth could say any more. They breezed past the two girls.

"We're off. Paula's nearly finished for the night and Toni needs her beauty sleep. I'm opening up early tomorrow, Beth." Rob passed a dramatic hand through his hair and Antonia waved at them as they both swept on.

Gary came back through the green room, plug in hand. No one spoke.

Jo went on pouring out her coffee as if Beth hadn't spoken. Then she said calmly, "The smell wasn't Beanie that time. My talc's intact and I certainly don't have any more stephanotis scent." She sipped in silence for a moment. Normally she would have poured a coffee for Beth as well.

A lead weight sat somewhere in the vicinity of Beth's heart, mingled with an overwhelming confusion. Jo *must* be protecting someone. That had to be Sam. Partly because he was Sam and mostly because he held her secret and she knew he wouldn't hold it for long if he felt cornered. Had they planned it together? After all, it was Sam who had hurled . . . all her thoughts were madness.

"I've had enough," she said. "Let's go home. Jo, please come with me."

Jo shrugged as if it didn't matter either way. "OK. Wait here and I'll pack up."

Cheryl, Toby and Sam clattered down from the stage and burst into the green room.

"To Mac's!" Sam shouted. "Ladies, your carriage awaits without!"

"Without us," Beth said. Jo had gone next door.

"Oh really?" Cheryl sounded surprised but not disappointed.

"Nope." Beth was watching Toby. She longed for him to say in his old way, "Oh, come on, SAPS against the world and all that." But he didn't. His face was closed to her, and he had his arm round Cheryl.

Dramatic to the last, Sam quoted, "Farewell! God knows when we shall meet again . . ."

"See you tomorrow, Sam," Beth said without a smile. Sam shrugged in mock despair. The others pushed him out. "Goodnight, goodnight . . ." floated back down the passage.

Rage at them all overwhelmed Beth without warning. Why should she give a damn whether they were killers or not!

Paula came in to do the last round with her keys, followed closely by Gary. He flashed Beth a look and left.

"Hello, Beth!" Paula smiled at her. "Still here?"

"Yes!" Beth said, still angry.

"Anything the matter?" Obviously Beth's tone had startled her. "Can I help?"

"Yes," Beth said again, her voice still hard. "As a matter of fact you can. Can I speak to you sometime?"

"About *Bella*? Is there something worrying you?"

"Not *Bella* exactly. Mr Lamb."

Paula drew her to a chair and sat beside her.

"Tell me, Beth. I won't say anything to anyone unless you want me to. You can trust me. Have you found out something?"

Beth suddenly felt very tired. Her rage against them all began to crumble. Face to face with a concerned, unknowing Paula she didn't know where to start. She began to wish she hadn't begun this.

"Jo's going to come back in a second . . ." Beth wiped a hand round her weary face, pushing back her hair. Paula looked at her exhausted stage manager.

"We'll find a moment tomorrow. You're flattened, Beth, and you've done such good work today. We got through a lot thanks to you. Can it wait?"

Beth nodded, grateful and relieved. By tomorrow she'd have had time to consider if telling Paula was the right thing to do.

Jo came back.

"Well done, Jo!" Paula got to her feet. "Everyone looks just right. Home now, girls."

Blast! I meant to tell her about the mess in the boiler room, thought Beth as they walked, in silence, to collect her basket. Paula ought to know about it. But she knew she didn't have the energy to go into all that now. Tomorrow would be soon enough.

There was no sign of the shattered bust of Queen Victoria in the scene dock. Someone had got rid of all the pieces. Beth touched her bruised shoulder tenderly. Whoever had wrecked the boiler room and thrown the bust from the prop gallery, where it had sat harmlessly for years, was either very strong or had the maniacal strength of a mind in torment. Either way, madness or sheer wickedness, it sent shivers through her. It had got too dangerous to keep all the secrets now. Rather than go to Paula, Beth agonized, she should go to the police.

Toby. The thought struck at Beth like a sword blade. He was behaving as if he really wished her ill. Was she getting too close to something he wanted hidden? She had forced him to confide in her – or that was how it felt to her now – and he was regretting it.

She alone knew that Baa-Baa had the power to wreck his happiness and home-life in one fell swoop. He wasn't a very strong personality anyway.

His early life had scarred him badly and now, thanks to Gary, Beth knew that he actually had a police record.

There was no denying he'd had the best opportunity to put the deadly weight in their bucket of blood. Had obsessive guilt, then, compelled him to return to Lamb's sanctum? And had he then sacked it in a blind rage? It was Toby who had seen her reading something there, she was sure – perhaps he even thought it was his poems! That was why he'd tried to put her out of action or frighten her so she couldn't go any further. He thought she'd found his love poems to Paula Barton!

She couldn't tell Paula about this, but she couldn't tell the police, either. Toby wasn't going to be betrayed by her, and that was that.

They unlocked their bikes.

Jo spoke, her voice flat. "Beth, will you really tell the police what you know?"

"No."

Beth could sense Jo's feeling of relief. When her friend spoke again it was with her old, loved voice.

"I've been . . . it's been . . . how are you, Beth? You said you'd been hurt. Are you all right?"

Beth let out a deep sigh as she felt tears of relief prick her eyelids. Her Jo was back. They slowly cycled out of The Tree's car park, side by side.

"I will be. I'll tell you about it later. It's just . . . the boiler room . . . the beastly stephanotis . . .

and," she gave a weak laugh, "the dratted bust of Queen Victoria!"

Jo knew her well. "And also?"

"And also . . . Toby's a bit . . . odd."

"Ah!" said Jo.

15

They were halfway through the technical rehearsal for *Bella* before Beth remembered that Mr Lamb's scrapbook was still stuffed into her dressing-table drawer.

With Jo sharing her room there hadn't been time to get it out to look at. Anyway, the girls had been so exhausted that they'd collapsed thankfully into bed as soon as they'd eaten the casserole Mrs Greene had kept warm for them. They were even too tired to speak very much to one another.

Beth's dreams were full of faces. The Bag Killer's victims' smiling faces merged and changed into masks of terror and she woke up sweating. When she slept again other faces took their place. Everyone's faces were just masks. Toby, Fiona, Paula,

Sam, Cheryl loomed towards her and each one removed their "mask" to reveal the face of Mr Lamb. It was frightful and Beth was glad when morning came.

Now, back at The Tree, she was grateful to have the play take her over again.

Before the rehearsal began Paula took her regular tour of inspection around the gantry, up the steep ladder-like steps at the prompt side and along the edge of the stage to the back, then across the width of the stage where the gantry became a bridge connecting one side to the other. This was high and narrow, and protected by a waist-high railing. Very few SAPS had authority to cross by it to the other side unless experienced or with an instructor. The op. prompt side of the gantry mirrored the other and ended with a similar flight of steps into the op. prompt corner, the only difference being that there was less room to manoeuvre on that side. It was an excellent facility for a little theatre, as long as it was used with care. Paula was very careful about this. No one wanted an accident with the lights.

The technical rehearsal got underway, with the actors just walking their parts, stopping now and then for Gary to alter his lighting plot to suit the action. It was important that everybody's face was lit so as to be seen clearly by the audience, no matter where they were on the stage. The performances weren't important, just scene changes, music cues, lighting and any other technical business the play required. The trap worked smoothly and Beth brought the final curtain down with a satisfactory swish.

"Not bad," was Paula's verdict, "but very slow scene changes. Beth, for goodness' sake get your team going a bit faster. The audience will go to sleep."

"Mind you," she told Beth afterwards, "it's not your fault if they've all got two left feet."

Somewhat to Beth's relief, Paula was too preoccupied to tackle Beth about their proposed talk.

The start of the dress rehearsal got later and later. Two o'clock came and went. It was a lot to ask of a cast, who were putting on complicated Victorian costumes as well as doing their make-up for the first time.

At three-thirty Beth, her props in place and the scenery up for the first Act, went to see if she could help Jo and her dressers.

There was pandemonium in the long room and hardly space for another body, so she left quickly and went next door.

Antonia was quietly seeing to her make-up for plain Ellen Porter. Fiona was panicking. Nostradamus was lost.

"Help me! Somebody help me," she was wailing. "I'll never remember a line if I can't find him. I'll wreck the whole play! We won't be able to open!"

Sam was dressed and ready even though he didn't come on till the third Act.

"Your ego, Fiona dear, is enormous." He spoke calmly, making no attempt to search for the missing mascot. Beth could see a little piece of leather thong sticking out from his cravat. He had his crystal, though.

Oh, Sam, you're too much, she thought silently.

Cheryl pinned a stray lock of hair back into her bonnet as Jo did up the row of tiny buttons down her back. At another part of the mirror Toby, fingers covered in grease, was desperately trying to flatten his hair.

Beth trod on something small and squashy. She bent down to look. It was Nostradamus.

Fiona squealed with joy and pounced on it, thrusting the little frog into her bodice.

"Angel!" she told Beth extravagantly. "Now I'm ready to give my all!" She twirled around in her excitement, making her long skirts swirl about her.

Toby's make-up box tipped to the floor, knocked off the table by a passing frilled petticoat.

"Fiona, you pest!" He stamped his foot with frustration and one side of his hair escaped the grease and stood on end.

"I'll do it," said Beth quickly. "Just everybody carry on. There's about five minutes to go."

Concentration deepened. Moustaches were stuck on, powder was applied and wet white rubbed into hands so that they would match faces when they were under stage lights. Beth, thankful to be useful, went down on her hands and knees to retrieve Toby's make-up sticks and cotton buds.

Her hand closed on something that wasn't a stick of face paint. It was a little glass phial with a cork stopper. Beth put it to her nose – stephanotis. The smell was now engraved on her senses. The little phial was empty.

Stephanotis! The last strand fell into place. Had Baa-Baa's episode with Cheryl finally tipped Toby over the edge? Or had Baa-Baa decided the time had come to show Toby's poems to his father and had Toby seized the chance to stop him? That was more likely.

Toby had carried the bucket up to the gantry and had had all the time in the world to put the weight in it. The stephanotis stuff was intended as some sort of smokescreen. He had access to all parts of the theatre. He had done it all.

She remembered the plaster bust flying at her. Her bruised shoulder was hurting now.

He must be close to madness, Beth thought. That's why he looks so calm. What on earth shall I do? I can't wreck *Bella*. I might be wrong, and then what?

She put the empty phial back in the make-up box among the sticks of grease paint and returned the box to the table.

For a moment Toby's eyes met hers in the large mirror. He looked away quickly, but not before Beth had seen a slightly startled expression in them.

I've got to be careful, she thought, sucking in her breath. I've got to look normal too. He mustn't suspect that I know.

The intercom crackled. "Beth, to your corner, please." Rob's disembodied voice drifted into the room.

Jo squeezed her shoulder. "Good luck!" Beth flinched. Wrong shoulder!

"Good luck, Toni! Good luck!" she called, and made for the stage. Only one thing was important now.

"Beginners, please!" Beth spoke into the microphone. It was always a thrilling moment. Those words had started shows in countless theatres down the ages. This was only the dress rehearsal but it still had the same effect. Beth saw the actors slip onto the stage.

"House lights!" she cued Gary and the auditorium slowly darkened.

"Overture!" The music came sweeping out. It too was controlled from the lighting box.

"And curtain," she silently cued herself and the dress rehearsal began.

It was a disaster.

Everything that could go wrong did. By the end

the actors were so rattled that they lost their lines and Rob, on the book, was going frantic.

Helpless to do anything about it, Beth tried to tell herself that a bad dress meant a good first night, but her hair was sticking to her neck with perspiration and she was as near to panic as she had ever been.

Concentration was very difficult. Watching Toby acting so normally and knowing what she knew about him split her down the middle.

Lights failed or cues were missed and the actors sounded off into darkness when they were meant to be having passionate encounters. Music interrupted serious speeches, props went missing, flats wobbled and the whole thing was half an hour too long.

Beth brought the curtain down, wanting to run away. Instead she said, "Everybody on stage!" into her mike.

Paula stood up. She had watched it all in silence.

"Do you really think we can ask the public to give good money to see this?" she asked them flatly.

Her group of actors looked at their feet, dejected.

"We've had weeks of rehearsal. There's no excuse for sloppy lines and missed cues. The stage staff don't have a lot of time to master a complicated set-up, that's true, but they've done only slightly better. Beth is a first-class stage manager, otherwise we'd still be doing Act Two." She let all that sink in and went up on to the stage with them.

"Now," she relented a little, "not even Fiona can blame all this on Bella's ghost."

They gave half-hearted grins. "But I know you can all do so much better or I'd cancel everything this minute. I won't give you lots of notes tonight. Just all go home, check your lines and have a good sleep.

"Beth and Gary," Paula's eyes searched for them, "we'll have the morning to run through everything before the show. Go, everyone," she said, "and sleep well."

The actors trailed downstairs to take off their make-up and costumes. Jo went to help.

Beth had moved over to tell the scene-shifters that they'd change back to the Act One set in the morning, when Paula came up.

"Beth, I truly hate to ask you this," she said, "but I noticed that there were gaps in the masking between a couple of flats and that the inside of the fireplace wasn't painted. Could you stay for half an hour and do it? I'd feel so much better if I knew you were doing it after this – débâcle."

Beth didn't hesitate. "Sure," she said.

"Shall I ask Toby to stay too?" Paula looked so apologetic.

"Oh, I expect he ought to be checking his lines,"

Beth said, hoping her voice sounded normal. She wasn't sure if she could ever be alone with Toby again. She wondered what his next move would be. He frightened her now. She'd be safer alone.

"I'm OK, Paula," she said aloud. "I've done it so many times. Shall I lock up after?"

"If you would," Paula looked grateful. "I promised to be somewhere tonight, or I'd . . ."

"No problem." Beth spoke firmly.

"And Beth," Paula added as she picked up her things, "I haven't forgotten about our talk. After the first night's over, eh?"

"OK." Beth left it at that. That problem was beyond her now.

The stage cleared quickly, leaving the set for Bella's death scene standing under the harsh white working light.

Beth moved towards the scene dock to get the paint and the strips of canvas needed for the jobs Paula had outlined. The chatter and bustle backstage had begun to thin out as SAPS departed. Sam, Fiona and the mob rushed past her. Gary was there too.

"See you in Mac's!" Cheryl waved to her as they left. She was holding Toby's hand. Look, folks! I've bagged the leading man, she seemed to be saying.

I'm not sure I care any more, thought Beth, watching Toby's tall figure out of sight. But she did care.

Jo came up, but Beth moved away from her, her eyes blurred with tears she couldn't stop.

"Paula says you're staying," Jo said. "Is there much to do?"

Beth fought for control. "Not really. I could have done it tomorrow but I didn't think to say. Paula must be anxious after the cock-up today, so I'll just get on with it." It'll be something positive to do, anyway, she added to herself.

"Dad's in his van outside or I'd stay too," Jo said.

"You go. I'm fine." Beth knew she was pushing Jo away, but her grip on herself was so borderline, even Jo's concern was threatening to break it up.

Jo looked at her uncertainly. "'Bye, then," she said and went.

I'm not going to have a friend left soon if it goes on like this, Beth thought miserably, watching the scene dock door close behind Jo's familiar back.

"Oh, pull yourself together!" she said out loud. "There are things to do." She made her way back to the stage, her hands full of the things she needed for the jobs that Paula had outlined, and tried to concentrate on the tasks ahead.

She walked towards the fireplace in the far side of the stage. The set was a Victorian theatre drawing room set like the one they were using a hundred years ago on the night when Bella Gardoni fell to her death.

Beth started to paint quickly, trying to shut out

the cavernous space of the empty auditorium that stretched away from her into infinity. Under the working lights and completely surrounded by darkness she felt as if she were the only person left in the world.

I don't usually feel as bad as this, she thought. Come on, Beth, she rallied herself. But her poor nerves were stretched to breaking point.

There was a tiny noise up in the flies – almost nothing, but it made her drop her brush and spatter the hearth rug with spots of black paint.

"Damn!"

There was silence. She mopped up with a scrap of cloth. Paint splashes, blood splashes – what's the difference? She gasped – there it was again. This time it came from the wings behind her, the prompt side.

"Now I'm hearing things, I hope . . ." She listened hard.

Again it came. A light tap, followed by another, until a rhythm of little sounds began . . . tap . . . tap . . . tap . . .

Huddled on her knees on the stage Beth rocked backwards and forwards. "Oh, God!" she moaned to herself. "I'm so frightened."

She knew she had to get up and see what was making the noise, but she didn't want to . . . she didn't want to . . . what if it wasn't a ghost? What if . . . what if she knew who it was? . . . and the

gentle tapping went on . . . and on . . . tap . . . tap
. . . tap . . . tap . . .

With a jerk Beth pulled herself up. Ready or not,
she thought, here I go.

She reached the wings in three strides and peered
through the dim light. She could see a lash-line
gently flipping against the metal railing above her
head. Trying desperately to see what was moving
it, she followed the line upwards until it disappeared into the darkness overhead. Then high
above her came a different sound; not a tap, more
of a scrape, followed by a flash of light. It was
reflected light from the front glass of a spot – one
of the large spots Gary had fixed to the gantry rail
that morning.

Some sixth sense made Beth jump backwards as
the huge light crashed down to fall heavily at her
feet, its glass shattering as it rolled a little and then
stopped still. The spotlight had tipped forward as it
fell and its glass had caught, for an instant only, a
glancing reflection from the working light. It had
acted as a warning.

The crash it made as it hit the stage was dreadful.
It shocked Beth into action. Someone, not a ghost,
was up there.

She darted up the gantry steps and along the side
of the stage to the back and saw a shadowy figure
turn the corner on the other side. Beth sped across
the gantry bridge in pursuit. She knew it well and

by the time the flying figure reached the steps on the other side of the stage she was gaining.

The figure in front half fell down the steps to reach the stage. Beth was so close behind that she knew they would be cornered when they reached the ground. It was impossible to turn quickly there. They would be safely trapped in the op. prompt corner.

She was.

With her back against the proscenium wall, Paula Barton turned at bay.

Beth wedged her in the corner, using her body and arms to fill the small gap between iron steps and theatre wall. Both were panting for breath.

Beth recovered first. "Paula!" It was more of a breath than a word.

Paula was dressed in black from head to foot. She was wearing dark glasses. In the half light, full of inky shadows, she looked like a stranger. And yet there was something oddly familiar about her, familiar but . . . different.

With a quick gesture Paula took off her glasses. "Is it you, Beth?" She tried to sound relieved.

"You know it's me," Beth said slowly. "You asked me to stay, after all."

The enormity of what had happened began to fill her. "You tried to – hurt me." She couldn't quite say "kill".

"No, I . . ."

Beth's mind was racing. "You planned this. All the time you were taking the rehearsal and telling me how well I'd done, you were planning to really hurt me. How could you? What had I done to you?"

Paula was getting back her self-possession. "Oh, Beth, I think I've made a terrible mistake. Thank God you're all right. I'd never forgive myself if—" she broke off. "Can't we sit on the stage and I'll tell you about it?" She made a little move towards her.

"Stay there!" Beth looked grim. "This has got to do with Mr Lamb. It has to. If he was alive we wouldn't be here like this. Did you put the weight in the bucket, Paula?"

"No! Of course not!"

"You had the chance." Beth realized this was true. "You were in the prompt corner on the book that evening. Toby said you were fiercer than usual about the lines. You could have sneaked up the steps any time and slipped it into the bucket."

"Don't be ridiculous, Beth!" Paula sounded scathing. "I didn't even know it was up there." She saw Beth hesitate, trying to remember the sequence of events on that terrible Saturday evening.

"Beth, this is nonsense. You're exhausted after all that's happ—"

But Beth broke in. "I remember you went through the scene dock after I met you in the green room. That's where the blood was."

"The boys were just chatting when I went through. I didn't even see the bucket."

"They could *not* have been just chatting – they were plotting. You could have heard them easily."

"This is silly," said Paula. "The bucket wasn't even there. I wouldn't know what they were talking about, would I?"

Beth thought. The bucket was there. The boys were plotting. But Paula must have stayed out of sight – there was plenty of cover in the dock at the time. The boys would have said if they'd seen her pass through, so they hadn't. She must have waited till the coast was clear.

"Well, that's easy," she said. "I can ask the boys. They'll remember."

Paula's eyes flickered. "Now, Beth. For goodness' sake, let's just get out of here and talk this over. There's a show tomorrow, and you have a job to do. You're over-tired." A touch of gentle authority came back into her voice. "It's all been a terrible strain – on all of us," she added, putting a hand up to her eyes.

Beth tried another tack, sure now that Paula was lying, but to prove it she had to bluff. She had to lie herself.

Please God, let this work, she prayed.

"Cheryl heard you and Baa-Baa talking before everyone went home on Saturday night. She was hiding in the loos until they'd all gone." Beth watched Paula's mouth tighten and she knew she was on the right tack.

"She heard him say you'd left something important of yours in his boiler room. She said . . . you sounded very upset."

Beth was playing a long shot and she knew it. "Cheryl told me bits of what he was saying to you. What did he have on you, Paula? He sounded as if he was trying to get you back into his room. You told me you'd hardly ever been in there. That's not true, is it?"

Paula said nothing. For the first time she began to look defeated.

"You've known all along what it's like in there. Did he show you his scrapbooks?" Paula's eyes widened. Beth put in the knife. "Did you know how revolting Baa-Baa really was? Do you know anything about the Bag Killer?"

"Oh, stop it, stop it!" Paula suddenly shouted. "What do you know about anything, Beth? You're a baby. You're still wet behind the ears!"

Beth saw she was near to cracking up. She took a breath and pressed on.

"You do know something. You do. Did you take the newspaper from his desk? Did you break up his room? What were you looking for? Why was Baa-Baa obsessed with killers? What did he like about them? What was so special about the Bag Killer? Will the scrapbook tell me? I have it, you know!"

"Ahhhh . . ." Paula gave a dreadful cry. "He was a monster . . . a monster!" She cracked completely. Her voice made the old theatre echo.

Beth went cold with horror. She wasn't quite sure which part of her questioning had gone home – something certainly had.

Paula's anguished face seemed to blur and the face that had looked out from that smudgy newsprint photograph, the unhappy blonde with spiky hair, was in front of her. It was Paula. She was the Bag Killer's wife.

Paula sank down where she stood with her face in her hands. When she looked up again she looked as old as she had in the photograph.

"No one will ever know," she said dully, "what it was like to find out that the person you lived with, slept and ate with, the person you loved, was capable of doing what he did and then coming home to you as if he'd just been to work."

"Oh, Paula!" The enormity of the thought overwhelmed Beth. She crouched down beside her. "It must have been terrible," she said.

"It was a nightmare every single day. After they told me I tried to kill myself. I had to . . . be looked after for a long time. You see, Beth," Paula's unhappy eyes looked into hers, "I felt so . . . dirty for being close to him. Dirty's too soft a word. I felt – damned."

Beth couldn't speak.

"When I got better I began to try to make a new life for myself. My old headmistress helped me into the job at Tolford School. I changed my name and how I looked and tried to put it all behind. I wasn't doing too badly, was I?" She paused and smiled bitterly. "I love it here at The Tree. It's all I ever wanted for a job." Her face changed. "Then he found out."

"Baa-Baa?"

"He dug and dug away at it. He was obsessive about violence and the violent. I don't know exactly how he first got the idea about me – he kept studying those old photos – but his friend Gina Thompson came from where I used to live and he got her to ask questions. He never let go and she fell under his spell, stupid bitch!"

"Cheryl's Aunty Gina!" Beth whispered. "But what did he want? Being married to a murderer isn't a crime, and you were divorced."

"You must know that George Lamb wanted power over people more than anything else, Beth. You knew him. He simply said he'd tell everyone who I was if I didn't go and live with him. Him! He was obscene!" Paula shuddered.

"If he told it would mean the end of everything for me in Tolford. No one would want someone with my background as a teacher or," and she paused again, "as a friend." She leaned her head against the wall and closed her eyes wearily.

"He gave me an ultimatum on Saturday – give in to him, or he'd tell. You saw me in the green room just after. I had to stop him."

"So you did put the weight in the bucket." Beth hated saying it. She remembered Paula's white face in the green room.

"It was an impulse. I only meant to stun him and maybe scare him, I don't know. Anyway, I heard what the boys were planning, and you guessed the rest."

"Tell the police. You're sure to get off lightly if he was blackmailing you." Beth felt so sorry for her.

"It's goodbye to all this if I do, Beth – everything I've worked for with SAPS. Would you like that?" Paula rose to her feet slowly. Her hands hung limply by her sides and she looked done in.

Beth stood up too. They faced each other. No, thought Beth, none of us would like that. She remembered Paula's ever-ready counsel, her humour and understanding at times of stress, and she felt helpless.

"Beth," Paula put out her hand and Beth could feel her own hand rising to grasp it.

But it never got there. Beth's guard was down. Paula bent over like a steel wire and butted her hard in her stomach. Beth staggered backwards, caught off balance. Paula leaped on her and turned her briskly round, wrenching both Beth's arms behind her back until she was forced to bend double.

"Did you think," she hissed in Beth's ear, "I'd let anyone take all this away from me?" She gave Beth a vicious push. "Get up those steps, Beth Greene, or I'll bash your face in!" To show she meant it she banged Beth's head against the iron rungs.

Beth gave a choking cry. It was all she could do with her arms pinioned like that.

Paula continued, her mouth close to Beth's ear. "I saw you spying on me. I knew what you were up to, Miss Clever!" She was taller than Beth, and very strong.

"Up! Up! Up!" she said, shoving her from behind, the force of her body pinning Beth to the flight of steps. To escape the excruciating pain in her arms Beth was forced to move away from her, upwards.

"Paula, please let me go," Beth gasped.

But Paula spoke between clenched teeth as she pushed her on, "And when you're up, up, up, then you'll go down, down, down – only quicker!"

She's mad, Beth realized as the top of the gantry steps got closer and closer. When I get to the top perhaps I might have a chance. She must save her breath.

They were up. Paula, still with her vice-like grip on Beth's arms, yanked her round to face back down the steps. Beth knew she was helpless. She could only wait for Paula to give her the final push. A strangled gasp struggled out of her open mouth.

She shut her eyes.

Abruptly her arms went free. This is it, she thought, but no push came. Weak with shock and relief she nearly fell, but managed to lean drunkenly against the railing just in time. Her shaking knees gave way at last and she sat down.

Paula was making strange noises. Someone had his arm around her neck.

"Toby!" Beth whispered.

Two struggling figures swayed from side to side on the narrow gantry bridge. Paula fought like a tiger and Toby needed all his strength to hold her. With a desperate wrench she broke free and ran back to the steps, pushing Beth out of her way. Toby was blocking the path to the prompt side. There was only one way down to the stage for her to go. Toby glided back across the gantry bridge and Beth lost him in the darkness.

Silence fell. Beth was incapable of moving, her legs refused to work. Toby must be up there somewhere, she thought, and Paula, screened by Bella's scenery, was waiting for her chance to run.

The stillness was unbearable.

Beth couldn't stand it any more. She pulled herself to her feet. "What am I, man or hamster?" she said as she forced her legs to descend the steps.

Hearing her move, Paula bolted. She sprinted like a shadow across the stage to reach the exit on the other side. She never got there.

With a terrible scream she fell headlong into the open stage trap, hitting her head on the side of the trap as she went. Then The Tree was silent again.

Toby came out of the prompt corner shadows to stand by the side of the trap and look down into it.

Beth, holding her aching arms around her, joined him.

Neither of them were able to speak. Finally Toby whispered, "I had to do it, didn't I, Beth?"

She knew what he meant. "Yes," she said and slipped her hand into his. "Do you think she's dead?"

"I saw her move. I don't think so. Probably concussed."

"We'd better call an ambulance – and the police. Are you all right?"

He nodded dumbly. "Are you?"

"Yeah," Beth breathed. She was numb again.

With the feeling that she had been there before, she left the stage and crossed the dark auditorium on her way to the telephone in the foyer. This time she was not alone.

Beth and Toby sat on the edge of the stage with their arms around each other, waiting for the police to arrive. Paula had moaned once, but now was quiet.

"What made you come back?" Beth asked Toby, very glad he had.

"It was an impulse thing," he said, and paused. "I hated the way things were going . . . the way we were behaving to each other. I wanted to have it out with you."

Beth thought about it. Everything before that last half-hour seemed a million years ago. It wasn't going to be easy to tell him that she'd thought he was the murderer.

"It was finding out you were doing all that stephanotis stuff," she said.

"What do you mean, me?"

"Well, I found the phial in your make-up box."

"I put it there after I picked it out of your basket!" Toby began to sound indignant. "I was disgusted with you."

"My basket?"

"D'you mean it wasn't yours?"

"Toby Harris," said Beth, "if you think I would do such a thing . . ." she broke off. She had thought he'd done something much worse than that.

"Fiona!" they said together.

"She needs the limelight so badly," said Toby. They thought about it. "When Paula got really angry with her she tried to dump the evidence. Anyway, the bottle was empty."

"Toby," Beth said slowly. "I've just remembered something. She felt the goose pimples begin on her arms. "I've remembered the very first time I smelt that perfume."

He looked at her.

"It was when I went through the green room just before I found Baa-Baa's body. Before anybody knew anything about it."

Toby looked at her thoughtfully. "Perhaps you're the fey one, after all?"

"No, not me. But you know, the time Fiona's face got scratched, she did go all odd and tell me I had to be careful as I was in grave danger. She said my aura looked awful!"

They couldn't help smiling, but it had been true.

"Hmmm," Toby said. "Did she do that scratching to herself, d'you think?"

"Oh, I doubt it. Someone didn't want her to go on dabbling the way she was – seances and things. It was meant to scare her off. She was right, it was a warning – for her, not SAPS. We may never know, but I guess it was Paula. Fiona sat up in the circle a lot and Paula's office is – was – up there."

They sat in silence for a moment, each wondering what SAPS was going to be like without her.

"Fiona saved my life," said Beth suddenly. "If we hadn't rowed and you hadn't come back to have it out with me . . ."

"Don't go on," Toby said.

"What did Cheryl think about you leaving her like that?" Beth chanced her arm.

Toby smiled at her. "Come on, Beth," he said, affection wrinkling up his eyes. "You and I go deeper than that, don't we? Cheryls will come and Cheryls will go, but we," he paused and held her gently by her shoulders, "are friends – the real thing."

"Friends," Beth sighed happily. "That's all right, then."

Two policemen came up through the prompt side entrance.

"Hello, SAPS!" said the one with ginger hair and freckles. He looked at Beth and smiled. "In trouble again?"

"We've got a lot to tell you, PC Daniels," she said.

The ambulance men arrived. "Can we bring her up on the trap?" Mark Daniels asked them. "I've always wanted to work this," and he pulled the lever.

Paula's limp body rose with the trap floor and lay on the stage. Beth and Toby stared at her familiar figure. She meant so much to us all, thought Beth, stealing a glance at Toby.

He was wondering how he was going to tell his father. He thought of the way his dad had lovingly restored the stage trap and done so much for the old Tree. Now the woman he loved lay unconscious on the same trap, a self-confessed murderer. For the first time that he could remember Toby felt pity for his father. He had been dealt a rotten hand.

They watched while Paula was expertly strapped on to a stretcher.

"Looks like a broken leg," one of the men said as they prepared to carry her away.

Beth and Toby were gathered up and taken to the police station, where they struggled to tell their stories.

DCI Armitage gave them a severe reprimand for holding back valuable information, but he wasn't too hard on them in the light of all they had gone through.

Beth felt very tired and her bruises had begun to ache badly.

"You're coming home in my Panda," said Mark Daniels.

"Yes, constable," said Beth with gratitude. She was beginning to get that special feeling again and wondered if he'd remember to ask her for the drink. She hoped so.

"SAPS against the world!" Toby said as he hugged her. "See you tomorrow, friend! We've got a show to do."

"Which," Beth smiled shakily at him, "as we know, must go on."

She sank gratefully down onto the little Panda's front seat and PC Daniels gently closed the door.